NEW YORK REVIEW BOOKS
CLASSICS

ENDING UP

KINGSLEY AMIS (1922–1995) was a popular and prolific British novelist, poet, and critic, widely regarded as one of the greatest satirical writers of the twentieth century. Born in suburban South London, the only child of a clerk in the office of the mustard-maker Colman's, he went to the City of London School on the Thames before winning an English scholarship to St. John's College, Oxford, where he began a lifelong friendship with fellow student Philip Larkin. Following service in the British Army's Royal Corps of Signals during World War II, he completed his degree and joined the faculty at the University College of Swansea in Wales. *Lucky Jim*, his first novel, appeared in 1954 to great acclaim and won a Somerset Maugham Award. Amis spent a year as a visiting fellow in the creative writing department of Princeton University and in 1961 became a fellow at Peterhouse College, Cambridge, but resigned the position two years later, lamenting the incompatibility of writing and teaching ("I found myself fit for nothing much more exacting than playing the gramophone after three supervisions a day"). Ultimately he published twenty-four novels, including science fiction and a James Bond sequel; more than a dozen collections of poetry, short stories, and literary criticism; restaurant reviews and three books about drinking; political pamphlets and a memoir; and more. Amis received the Booker Prize for his novel *The Old Devils* in 1986 and was knighted by Queen Elizabeth II in 1990. He had three children, among them the novelist Martin Amis, with his first wife, Hilary Anne Bardwell, from whom he was divorced in 1965. After his second, eighteen-year marriage to the novelist Elizabeth Jane Howard ended in 1983, he lived in a London house with his first wife and her third husband.

CRAIG BROWN is the author of *Hello Goodbye Hello*, *The Lost Diaries*, and *The Marsh-Marlowe Letters*. He writes a weekly book review for *The Mail on Sunday*, a twice-weekly column for *The Daily Mail*, and for the past twenty-five years has written a parodic diary for *Private Eye* magazine.

OTHER BOOKS BY KINGSLEY AMIS
PUBLISHED BY NYRB CLASSICS

The Alteration
Introduction by William Gibson

Girl, 20
Introduction by Howard Jacobson

The Green Man
Introduction by Michael Dirda

Lucky Jim
Introduction by Keith Gessen

The Old Devils
Introduction by John Banville

One Fat Englishman
Introduction by David Lodge

Take a Girl Like You
Introduction by Christian Lorentzen

ENDING UP

KINGSLEY AMIS

Introduction by
CRAIG BROWN

NEW YORK REVIEW BOOKS

New York

THIS IS A NEW YORK REVIEW BOOK
PUBLISHED BY THE NEW YORK REVIEW OF BOOKS
435 Hudson Street, New York, NY 10014
www.nyrb.com

Library of Congress Cataloging-in-Publication Data
Amis, Kingsley.
 Ending up / Kingsley Amis ; introduction by Craig Brown.
    pages ; cm. — (New York Review Books Classics)
 ISBN 978-1-59017-759-4 (pbk.)
 I. Title.
 PR6001.M6E5 2015
 823'.914—dc23

                             2014029156

ISBN 978-1-59017-759-4
Available as an electronic book; ISBN 978-1-59017-797-6

Printed in the United States of America on acid-free paper.
10 9 8 7 6 5 4 3 2 1

Introduction

Irritation is generally considered a minor emotion, less noble than anger, less operatic than rage. Over the centuries, it has inspired no great poem, speech, or drama, though it may have prevented quite a few from seeing the light of day.

But in Kingsley Amis's *Ending Up*, irritation is raised to the level of art. Just as his old friend Philip Larkin thought that "deprivation is for me what daffodils were to Wordsworth," so Amis's daffodils were irritation. He was both irritable and irritating, equally adept at feeling intense irritation and dishing it out.

His first wife, Hilly, noticed Amis's remarkable two-way capacity in this area soon after they first met at Oxford in 1946, when he was just twenty-three years old. From the start, she was aware of his "endless complaints about what seemed to me harmless things like apparently ordinary, nice people going through the swing-door at Elliston's restaurant. He'd start muttering, 'Look at those fools, look at that idiot of a man,' and so on. If doors got stuck, or he was held up by some elderly person getting off a bus, or the wind blew his hair all over the place, he would snarl and grimace in the most irritating fashion."

As a young novelist, he seemed to know instinctively how to channel this curse into prose. Throughout his oeuvre, irritation plays on the Amis landscape like sun on sea. His first novel, *Lucky Jim* (1954), bristles with it. Its antihero, Jim Dixon, lacks any sort of capacity for brushing things off. "He wished this set of dances would end; he was hot, his socks seemed to have been sprayed with fine adhesive sand, and his arms ached like those of a boxer keeping his guard up after fourteen rounds." Figures in authority, notably his professor, are particularly annoying. "Welch's driving seemed to have improved slightly; at any rate, the only death Dixon felt himself threatened by was death from exposure to boredom."

Subsequent Amis novels extend the boundaries of irritation to form something approaching an empire. "It was no wonder that people were so horrible when they started life as children," observes the protagonist in *One Fat Englishman*. More often than not, Amis's characters are drawn into a spiral of irritation at themselves. "Feeling a tremendous rakehell, and not liking myself for it, and feeling rather a good chap for not liking myself much for it, and not liking myself at all for feeling rather a good chap," observes the narrator of *That Uncertain Feeling*.

But it was not until he was well into middle age that Amis decided to pluck irritation from the chorus line and place it center stage. For some time, he had been living in the countryside outside London with a slightly ragtag group of people: his second wife, the novelist Elizabeth Jane Howard; her brother Colin, known as Monkey; and Monkey's artist friend Sargy Mann. For three years, they had been joined by Jane's mother, Katherine "Kit" Howard, "an unhappy woman with a sharp tongue, not an easy presence in the household for anyone," in the words of Amis's biographer.

One day, Jane wondered aloud what would happen "if we all went on living together and grew old together." With these words, she planted the seed for *Ending Up*. Interviewed by Clive James after the novel was published in 1974, Amis said that the idea had come from his own experience: "What would this sort of arrangement be like if one had a pack of characters who were all about twenty years older[?]" He had imagined "a situation where everybody was old, everybody had got to the end of their lives, and everybody had been there for a good long time so that all knew how boring one another was, and exactly the areas where one another was most vulnerable."

Before he embarked on writing *Ending Up*, on January 29, 1973, Amis compiled eight pages of notes, kicking off with a list of forty-five "ways of being annoying," each of which pops up in the novel. Alongside each different way, he added one of five letters, indicating the character who would best personify it: A for Perverse Shag (Adela),

B for Egotist (Marigold), X for Shit (Bernard), Y for Fool (Shorty), and
Z for Bore (George). Thus:

> X Being deaf—the which?—contemptuous when told
> Z Talking quietly, then v. loudly
> Y Repeating the wrong bit
> A Telling people to do what they'll do anyway & what they know
> A Wrong end of stick through eye of needle
> X Anger at simple questions
> B Whining—I'm old, on scrap-heap
> Y Punning<,> dud spoonerisms
> Y Polysyllabic facetiousness
> B Lying about what's happened, whose side was on in argt.

And so forth. He then wrote suitably merciless short biographies for
each of the five characters, such as:

> A <Adela> (72). X's sister. Never married (too ugly, but really
> too boring or annoying). Ex-matron. Runs house....

and:

> B <Marigold> (74) A's oldest friend. Widow. Ex-"actress." Has
> children. Hates X & Y. Laxative (for Y). Rt wing. Hates homos,
> lefties, nig nogs, EEC ... Makes convenience of A, enjoys show-
> ing herself superior to her. Upper class. Amnesia just starting.

Alongside X for Bernard (76), who was to become the pivotal character, Amis wrote: "Old queer but has child. Deaf. Malicious. Amnesiac.
Hates everyone. Telephone wire for B. Heated wine for Y. Funny. 'Bad
leg.' Dying & knows it. Waterpistols cats. India (for laxative). Can't
drink. Small pension. Reads. Not enough to do."

Amis's method seems to have been to gather forty-five ways of
being annoying from the inhabitants of his own home, and then to
redistribute them, in roughly equal proportions, among his fictional
characters. For instance, he told his official biographer, Eric Jacobs,

that Jane's most annoying characteristic was primarily conversational. "Amis would ask Jane a question and instead of answering she would ask why he'd asked it, as if nothing could be straightforward, not even a simple question."

This tic reappears in the conversation of Marigold. Unlike Marigold, Jane was never an actress, but she used to complain to Amis that the publisher Victor Gollancz could never remember who she was, and always mistook her for an actress, a mistake Amis could understand, given that she was, he said, so "affected."

Cruel, perhaps, but he was crueler still in his characterization of Bernard, who appears to be an exaggerated and accelerated version of Amis himself. John Cleese once remarked that every young comic plays the character he dreads becoming. At the age of fifty, Amis was far from young, but his portrait of Bernard is surely a projection of all his most objectionable tendencies, amplified by old age. The only joy Bernard is able to extract from life is in making it worse for others: "his only relief, and that a mild, transient one, had turned out to lie in malicious schemes, acts and remarks."

In 1971, Amis said, "If you can't annoy somebody with what you write, I think there's little point in writing." His most thorough biographer, Zachary Leader, suggests that "the desire to irritate and annoy animated Amis all his life"; *Ending Up* represents the most extravagant, unbridled, and, it must be added, hilarious animation of this perverse desire.

What do they think has happened, the old fools,
To make them like this? Do they somehow suppose
It's more grown up when your mouth hangs open and drools,
And you keep on pissing yourself, and can't remember
Who called this morning?

Larkin finished his poem "The Old Fools" just over a fortnight before Amis began writing *Ending Up*. The two works share an almost rapturous sense of disgust at the various afflictions of old age—fear, panic, incontinence, amnesia, paralysis.

"One thing the book isn't going to be is a serious, in-depth etc, study of old age," Amis wrote to an interviewer when he was roughly halfway through. "It's about five particular people who wouldn't be behaving as they do if they weren't old."

The finished product is short and brutal, a series of cackling vignettes of man's cruelty to man, all conveyed in Amis's crisp, beady prose. It is also very funny, growing funnier with each fresh misery, mishap, and atrocity. The blurb on my Penguin edition draws attention to its "humanity" but it might more accurately have high-lighted its inhumanity: Few novels have ever been quite this bleak, quite this nasty. Even the pets at Tuppeny-hapenny Cottage become embroiled in the general unpleasantness, in a manner that mirrors their masters: "Mr Pastry and Pusscat were locked in their peculiar form of combat, one that started as a mixture of fight and game in about equal proportions, with an escalating trend in favour of the fight element."

Amis's well-loved misanthropy had never been so extreme. When an interviewer from *The Paris Review* suggested it was "very bleak," he replied:

Yes, well, no book is the author's last word on any subject, or expresses what he feels all the time. So if I were to walk under a bus this afternoon, then *Ending Up* would be my last novel, and people might say, "Well, he ended in a fit of pessimism and gloom." This wouldn't really be so. Each novel can only repre-sent a single mood, a single way of looking at the world, and one feels bleak from time to time, and takes a fairly pessimistic view of one's own future and chances. But there are other times when one doesn't, and out of that other books emerge.

Yet it is to my mind one of the funniest of his novels, its pessimism refined and polished so that it glistens with glee. It is also one of his most irresistibly inventive, as he employs the verbal tics of each differ-ent character to create a succession of conversational cartwheels, most notably with poor old George, who, following a stroke, suffers from nominal aphasia and is always groping for the right word. "Did you watch, you know, the thing on the switching it on last night?" he says. He means television.

On its publication in the United States, *Ending Up* was reviewed glowingly in *The New York Review of Books* by Matthew Hodgart, who suggested that its author derived the novel's structure from a baroque suite or a classical work in sonata form, possibly Mozart's String Quintet no.4 in G minor K 516. Amis's response was characteristically blunt. "Is he mad?" he asked an American friend adding, "As far as I know I've never even heard that Mozart quintet. Still, the review certainly won't lose any sales."

Amis despised artists who gave themselves airs and made sure he never did it himself, much preferring to play the role of the anti-intellectual philistine. While writing *Ending Up*, he took issue with an article Frank Kermode wrote in *The Daily Telegraph* in celebration of Ezra Pound. "Few would deny he had genius," Kermode had proclaimed. In response, Amis wrote a letter to the editor: "No indeed; only it was a genius not for poetry (he had not even any particular talent in that direction) but for behaving sufficiently like a great poet to gull the gullible." Ten days later, Pablo Picasso happened to die, and Amis's reaction was much the same. "My dear Philip," he wrote to Larkin in April 1973, "So Pablo the piss-poor paint-pusher has fallen off the hooks at last, eh? Ho ho ho. Beckett next?"

Yet, despite its author's forthright denial, there remains something musical about *Ending Up*. It is an elaborate dance of death, the five main characters following the manic, fateful steps preordained by their flaws, right up to the moment when the music stops and they all collapse. But Amis's mischievous delight in language and the extreme brevity of his chapters also give the work a jaunty feel, so that the great somber themes of old age and death are transformed into the prose equivalent of a jig.

In one particular way, *Ending Up* proved eerily prophetic. Ten years later, Amis had, by all accounts, turned into an only slightly paler version of Bernard Bastable—grumpy, cussed, perversely devoted to causing offense. His sixtieth birthday, in 1982, was marked by *The Observer* newspaper with a dinner in his honor at the Garrick Club, attended by no fewer than four editors and five columnists. At the meal's end, the editor delivered a fulsome toast. In reply Amis stood up and said, "I just want to make a few remarks. The first thing I've got to say to you is *The Observer* is a bloody awful paper."

Julian Barnes had long been a friend and admirer of Amis, but as the years went by, he came to find the role increasingly difficult. "The price you had to pay for his company got higher. Every meeting would involve at least one remark, aside, riff at which you thought, well, I'm just not going to rise to that. It would be nignogs, it would be Jews, it would be women, it would be Irish, it would be gays. You would think, we'll let that pass, but increasingly... it seemed that the price to pay was swallowing what you believed about things."

Another example of life following art, of a prophesy fulfilled, came in Amis's last days, when this most articulate of men lay in a hospital bed, the power of language having all but deserted him, now more George Zeyer than Kingsley Amis.

—I feel a bit ... you know.
—What, Dad?
—You know.
—Anxious? Uneasy?
—Not really. Just a bit ... You know.

His son Martin writes movingly about it in his memoir, *Experience*. At one point, he asks Amis, "Do you remember the book you wrote called *Ending Up*?" and goes on to regale him with the wit and brilliance he applied to George's nominal aphasia.

—All this, Dad, in the book *you wrote*.
He is contemplating me with delighted admiration.
—Do you remember?
—No, he said.

— CRAIG BROWN

ENDING UP

To Betty and Paul Fussell

One

'How's your leg this morning, Bernard?' asked Adela Bastable.

'Much as it was yesterday morning,' said her brother in his usual bantering tone. 'Or afternoon, for that matter. Sorry, but there it is.'

'Because it's quite a long way from this new place to the car-park. From the supermarket itself, I mean. You have to come out at the front, where you go in, and go all the way round to the back. You'd think they'd have an entrance or an exit at the back, wouldn't you?'

'Or even both. In a sense, yes, you would. Why not go to the old place?'

'I've explained all that to you I don't know how often,' said Adela in her thick voice, one that seemed to make it hard for her to express by its tone any emotion but a mild resentment. 'We're getting poorer the whole time because of inflation, so I have to keep trying new places to see that we get the best value for money. If you took the slightest interest in the affairs of the household you wouldn't have to be told that.'

'Wouldn't I? Anyway, I do, don't I, Shorty? Take an interest in the affairs of the household. I can't help my leg.'

The man Bernard Bastable had spoken to was not short. Nor was he tall enough for the name to be appropriate as an irony. He was known as Shorty partly because his surname was Shortell, and partly because it was generally felt that his domestic status, not on a level with the others' and yet not properly that of servant, rather ruled out the use of his Christian name, which was Derrick. He said in a sort of Irish accent, although he was not Irish, 'Och, now, a course ya can't, me ould darlin. Ya can't go expectin a fella to—'

'I don't see what stops him taking an interest,' said Adela. 'Actually physically prevents him.'

3

'Shorty means to express his agreement with the proposition that I can't help my leg,' said Bernard, speaking as clearly as he could, which was not very clear. He still sounded rather drunk, but he was no more drunk than Shorty was Irish; he had not been drunk for fifteen years.

'How a bad leg prevents you from being able to carry things is a mystery to me.'

'Yes, I know it is. It's something of a mystery to me as well. And of course it's a complete mystery, hidden in total and impenetrable darkness, to Mainwaring. Or Maine-wearing, as he seems to think it's pronounced.' Bernard referred to the local doctor, one much despised and much in demand.

'Anyway, you can't come to the supermarket.'

'Only as a companion. Not as a carrier of things.'

'Look, I'll come, Adela,' said Shorty in his native modified-Cockney.

'No, Shorty, you're needed here. Don't forget that Trevor and Tracy are coming to luncheon, so you'll do the vegetables, won't you? And you'll clear up breakfast.'

'Shorty clears up breakfast every morning of his life.'

'Indeed he does. It's amazing how many things a bad leg can prevent one from doing.'

Bernard started reading the *Radio Times*, or his glance fell to it.

'There's bound to be a bloke there who'll carry your stuff, Adela,' said Shorty. 'Some kid or other.'

'They have to know you before they'll do that.'

'Yet one more argument for going to the old place,' said Bernard.

'I've already explained about that and I haven't the time or the inclination to run over it again.' Adela looked at her hefty wrist-watch. 'I must be off; I've got to go to the chemist and the cleaners as well. And I might be able to fit in the electricity shop too. We need a plug for that lamp. The one by the sitting-room window. I'll just have to see how things turn out. It's largely a question of the traffic. You just can't tell in advance. It seems to be quite unpredictable. Bernard.'

'What?'

'Bernard,' said Adela more loudly.

'I heard you say my name. I was asking in effect what you wanted, not for a repetition of what you had said. As my use of a falling rather than a rising inflection might have suggested.'

'Oh, honestly . . . You'll go in and see George, won't you?'

'What about?' Bernard seemed struck by unlooked-for possibilities.

'You know very well. Just see him.'

'Just seeing him would hold few enough attractions. Talking to him, which is what you mean, holds fewer still. Being talked to by him, that is.'

'I freely undertake to give you the undeniable support of my companionship in your charitable enterprise, Bernard,' said Shorty.

'Don't forget it's because of you he's here,' said Adela to Bernard.

'What?'

'Don't forget it's because of—'

'Oh, what nonsense,' said Bernard lightly. 'It was all your idea, as you well know.'

'In his condition . . . given his circumstances . . .' Adela's head moved about on its short neck as if she were looking for physical escape. 'He hadn't got anybody else. You must realize . . .'

'That bloody dog.'

'But you can't expect—'

'We all realize, Adela,' said Shorty. 'Even Bernard when he's not playing silly buggers. You go off now before the shops fill up. Go on.'

'When will you be back?' asked Bernard. 'In case some man comes or rings up or something.'

'I've told you: as soon as I've been to the supermarket and the cleaners and the—'

'When will you be back?'

'What o'clock is what the brigadier desires to be informed,' said Shorty.

Adela looked at her watch again. 'With luck, about twelve.'

'Ah,' said Bernard. 'Twelve-thirty. Ish.'

Two

Stumbling slightly over the threshold, Adela Bastable left Tuppenny-hapenny Cottage by its front door. The house, standing at the edge of a fair-sized tract of woodland and once, perhaps, the abode of gamekeepers, had been her and her brother's and Shorty's home for eleven years. Adela, to whom it had fallen to conduct all the dealings, had picked the place up cheap from an artistic couple who said they had found it too large for them. They might have added that they had also found it too cold in winter, in too much disrepair to be renovated except at great expense, and too isolated: three miles from the nearest village and nearly seven from the nearest town, Newmarket. Nobody would deliver milk or newspapers. So it had not been cheap in the sense of being a bargain, only in that of being what, for the new occupants, it had had to be – low in price and not actually uninhabitable. To Adela, it was a pretty house too, prettier than anywhere else she had ever lived, at any rate on the outside.

As always when leaving or returning, she paused now and looked up at the long, crooked façade with conscious pleasure. Eighteenth-century timber-frame was what she called the style of the house when asked, and sometimes when not. She would admit to herself that she was not really sure about either half of the description. The estate agent had been emphatic as to the period, but had turned vague, though staying emphatic, when asked to specify a date. It was her guess that the building had originally been called something else now left far behind by the flight of whim that had retitled it. The timber-frame issue was unclear too, in that there was not very much timber involved. But never mind: what with the quiet, the nearby woods and all their wild life, the results of Shorty's work in the garden, it was far from a bad place to end up.

She had been in the driver's seat of her 1967 Morris 1100 estate car for some little time before she realized that the ignition key, since it was neither in its socket nor in her handbag, must be on her dressing-table. Back in the house, she passed Bernard on his way to the sitting-room. He was limping heavily, but then he could have heard her come in. When she explained about the key, he said with a smile that it was a good idea to go and fetch it, because he had always found that cars worked better with their ignition switched on. Adela mounted the steep, creaking stairs. She wished, as she still occasionally found herself doing, that her brother would let her love him, but of course it was too late for that. It had been too late since they were children before the first war.

Finding somebody she could love had been the main quest of Adela's life until about the time of her fiftieth birthday, when its impracticability had become clear to her. The prospect of receiving love she had abandoned much earlier. She had never been kissed with passion, and not often with even mild and transient affection. This she explained to herself as the result of her extreme ugliness. She was a bulky, top-heavy woman with a red complexion, hair that had always been thin, and broad lips. To love somebody, she had found, was impossible unless something was given in return: not indeed love, nor so much as positive liking, but interest, notice. Her career in hospital catering, taken up after she had been told, without further explanation, that she was not the right type to become a nurse, had brought her into contact with thousands of people until her retirement in 1961. None of them had become her friend, in the sense that none had agreed to go to a theatre or a coffee-shop or a sale with her more than a couple of times, and so she had lived alone throughout her working life. Now, after Bernard had made his astonishing offer, that she could housekeep for him and Shorty, she was among people and, with all the difficulties this seemed inevitably to bring, happier than at any time since her childhood. Her only fear was of falling helplessly ill and having nobody to leave in charge; it was a comfort that Dr Mainwaring, whom she trusted in medical matters, had told her that her gastric ulcer, while bringing her occasional bouts of pain and nausea, was under control, and that she was otherwise in good condition for a woman of seventy-one.

The Morris lurched and swung its way along the fifty yards of unmade track to the road. She must tell Shorty to have another go at filling in the pot-holes, which seemed to reappear with every heavy fall of rain, such as the mid-autumn skies now threatened. Adela was late and would have to face the traffic and the crowds, but she knew she could manage that.

Three

'You'd be far better off *in* a home,' sang Shorty, vigorously running a wire pad round a frying-pan, vigorously enough to shorten its effective life by one per cent or so – 'you'd be far better off *in* a home . . .' He had picked up the tune in his Army days, and singing it was largely an unconscious habit. Not altogether: now and then the thought would recur to him that these words might pass for a comment on his situation in life, so Adela heard them from him fairly regularly. He sang them through again several times in the course of preparing the sprouts and potatoes and tidying up the little dark lopsided kitchen.

A good half of the space here was taken up by a bare rectangular table; farmhouse style, it was sometimes said, and whenever it was said Shorty would mutter to himself that the thing must have come from the part of the farmhouse they kept for the shower that shovelled the shit. The table had indeed a cheap, hasty look. Round it stood some upright chairs, no two the same, lone survivors of otherwise vanished sets. The china crowding the dresser showed further unplanned variety, also the cutlery drawer, in which Shorty laid the final egg-eroded teaspoon.

He went to work briefly on the floor with a broom, leaving some fragments behind among the irregularities of the tiles, shoving the majority through a useful crack under the sink. The pit beneath must fill up some day, but he reckoned it would last his time. After shaking the greasy rush mat in the outer doorway, he replaced it in front of the range, where a log fire burned. Really successful fires at Tuppenny-hapenny Cottage were far from the rule, but this one had never quite gone out for over two months, and was now well on the way to gaining a hold. He checked the gas-oven (the range was never hot enough for actual cooking) just as the clock above the mantelshelf, stolen by

8

him from a station waiting-room one drunken wartime night, struck the hour.

'Eleven ack-emma,' said Shorty. 'Time for a burn and a nip.' He took cheap cigarettes and a book of matches from the pockets of his navy-blue cardigan and, while lighting up, considered. How recently had he punished the bottle he kept behind the vacuum cleaner in the cupboard under the stairs? Probably not since the previous morning. He went and poured a good, a very good, half-tumbler of Dr Macdonald's, a proprietary mixture of Scotch whisky and British wine, and drank with a will. The taste he found rather unpleasant, but if he had found it pleasant he might be drinking more of the stuff and becoming incapable earlier in the day. It was cheap, too, and Adela never missed a chance of going on at everyone about the need for economy, always adding, with the show of fair play that gave him the pip so consistently, that she had no real right to go on at him, because he contributed more to the household budget than anybody else; and then sometimes adding, when they were alone, that at seventy-three he should drink less for his health's sake. Drink more for his age's sake, he would say to himself.

He topped up his glass and recapped and replaced the bottle, which was beginning to look a bit of a bloody fool after what he had done to it. To him, the point about this bottle was that Adela knew it was there and, if she judged only by the rate its contents disappeared, must form a falsely reassuring estimate of his daily intake. He imagined, wrongly, that she did not know he knew she knew the bottle was there and, also wrongly, that she did not know about the bottles respectively on top of his wardrobe, in his otherwise empty suitcase behind the box-room door, and among the gardening tools in the coal-house. Further, he kept forgetting, because of being drunk at the time, that the off-licence van normally brought him his fresh stocks at the end of its daily round, just when Adela would be in the kitchen making tea; so throwing a careful three-quarters of the empties away in the woods was labour wasted, except as exercise. The whole matter of Shorty, Adela and the bottles could be taken as, among other things, illustrating in him that strange, inseparable mixture of real, almost instinctive obedience and covert, largely futile disobedience which long Army service in the ranks so often creates. And Derrick Shortell's service had been long, from enlistment in 1914 as a boy soldier to discharge in 1945 with the rank of company quartermaster-sergeant, and an MM, and an unofficial gratuity of just under £12,000 from flogging petrol, meat etc. to civilians.

He felt a twinge at his anus. 'You are a sodding liar,' he said to it. 'Not an hour ago you were on about that was that for the day – what, you bother me again? not you, and butter wouldn't melt in your mouth. All right, fuck you, I'll go quietly. That bleeding wine. Thought Scotch was supposed to be binding.' His drink finished, he hurried outside and round the corner to the lavatory there. As always, it was a quick business. 'Not like poor old bloody Bernard,' said Shorty. 'Half an hour's nothing. Piles must be hell.'

Perhaps it was piles of unusual hellishness that had that morning intensified Bernard's always noticeable pallor. Entering the sitting-room a couple of minutes later, Shorty was struck by this and by how old it made the other look. Or rather, how extra old. His eyes were perpetually bloodshot and on the point of running over; half the flesh in his face seemed to have settled about and beneath the downturned lower lip; he was generally fat, again in a bottom-heavy way. More like eighty-five than seventy-five, thought Shorty, whereas he himself, with only a few wrinkles, an upright carriage and a lot of dark brown left in his hair, could pass for sixty-odd, at any rate when reasonably sober. In this he was correct. At moments like the present it struck him how hard it was to believe that, thirty-five years ago, on a couple of dozen occasions, he had let this man make love to him, and had enjoyed it; not hard to remember – that was all too easy – but hard to believe.

On the transistor radio, a woman was saying with conviction that you had to let the mixture marinate for at least two hours beforehand.

'You listening to this, Bernard?'

'What?'

'Are you listening to this?' asked Shorty more clearly.

'With inexhaustible fascination. No, in fact I'm waiting for something else to come on.'

'Is it important?'

'Of course not. Why?'

'I thought we might get George done.'

'Oh Christ, not now.'

'Either we get him done now, Bernard, you and me together, or you do him on your own while I go into the garden and plant some of those grape hyacinth bulbs for naturalizing. Or you don't do him at all and Adela gets to know. The decision,' ended Shorty in what he thought of as a half-crown accent, 'is entirely in your very capable hands, my dear fellow.'

'It's raining.'

'Not enough to bother me it isn't, and it's just right for the bulbs.'

'Bloody horticulture,' said Bernard in his slurred tones. 'All right. Let's go and do him.'

Four

George Zeyer, Emeritus Professor of Central European History at the University of Northampton, was lying in bed upstairs waiting to be done. In a different sense he had been done already, when Shorty had helped him to the bathroom and later back. Five months previously, George had had a severe stroke that had incapacitated him with hemiplegia, that condition in which the motor muscles of half the sufferer's body are paralysed. In this case, George being right-handed, it was the right half. He had come, or been brought, to Tuppenny-hapenny Cottage because, as Adela had observed earlier that morning, and many times earlier than that, he had had nowhere else to go, except into a hospital ward. Bernard, once the husband of his late sister, Vera, was his only surviving connection outside his native Bohemia, which he had not seen since the age of ten. Now, at an exact seventy, he was the youngest of the household, a small man who had often been called dapper in the past and was still handsome in his fashion. He had abundant white hair, clear eyes of an unusual light brown and a healthy skin.

Heralded by the groaning and popping of loose floor-boards,

Bernard and Shorty came into the small bedroom, which was damp but, thanks to an electric heater, not cold. George looked over his half-glasses at them and smiled with the left side of his face. Mr Pastry, however, gave an unsteady growl; his sight had been failing for some time and now, as he approached the age of sixteen, his sense of smell too might have started to weaken. He was a white bull-terrier cross, with short legs, a lot of pink on his muzzle, and an odour that was not so much unpleasant as disquieting in some way hard to define.

'Now now, you silly old thing, it's only kind Uncle Bernard and kind Uncle Shorty,' said Shorty. 'Hallo, George.'

'Yes, do be quiet, Mr Pastry.' George's voice was as indistinct as Bernard's, but not in the same style. 'If you go on behaving like that, people aren't going to want to know you. Just you pull yourself together. That's a good dog. We really can't have you interfering in the conversation. I should think so, too. Sorry, chaps – do sit down.'

'Thank you,' said Bernard, 'but when my leg's giving me gyp, as it seems determined to go on doing, I find standing up tends to help a little.'

'In that case, of course. I'm sorry you've been having a bad time.'

'How are you, George?' asked Shorty with some emphasis, seating himself on the walnut Queen Anne chair that George had formerly used at his desk.

'Oh, I've been all right, since we last met. I say, have you fellows seen about this?'

With his left hand, George tapped the copy of the *Daily Telegraph* that lay open in front of him on the plaid blanket. It was naturally the issue of the preceding day, naturally because of what had become a household custom. He liked a newspaper to read with his breakfast; the newspaper of any given morning did not arrive until Adela had fetched it from the village, and even after that was not available to him until Bernard, in particular, had quite finished with it. So George kept up with events twenty-four hours in arrears. To one who was interested in long-term movements of history rather than day-to-day occurrences, and who took the precaution of never listening to news broadcasts, the delay hardly mattered.

'Seen about what?' asked Bernard after a pause.

'This man Banda. Talking his head off again. Some trade agreement he evidently doesn't care for.'

'He hasn't been kidnapped, has he?' asked Shorty.

'It doesn't say so here. Was there something on the wireless?'

'Because if he had, it would be a Banda-snatch, wouldn't it? I worked that out the other day.'

Bernard wheeled towards the window as abruptly as if a terrorist had just that moment swung into view outside it.

'I suppose it would,' said George judicially.

'And they'd write the details up in a Banda-log.'

'Would they? Who?'

'Oh, some blokes round the place.'

'Well, anyway, to start with he must have a, a thing, you know, you go about in it, it's got, er, they turn round. A very expensive one, you can be sure. You drive it, or someone else does in his case. Probably gold, gold on the outside. Like that other chap. A bar – no. And probably a gold, er, going to sleep on it. And the same in his . . . when he washes himself. If he ever does, of course. And eating off a gold – eating off it, you know. Not to speak of a private, um, uses it whenever he wants to go anywhere special, to one of those other places down there to see his pals. Engine. No. With a fellow to fly it for him. A plate. No, but you know what I mean. And the point is it's all because of us. Without us he'd be nothing, would he? But for us he'd still be living in his, ooh, made out of . . . with a black woman bringing him, off the – growing there, you know. And the swine's supposed to be some sort of hero. Father of his people and all that. A plane, a private plane, that's it.'

It was not that George was out of his mind, merely that his stroke had afflicted him, not only with hemiplegia, but also with nominal aphasia, that condition in which the sufferer finds it difficult to remember nouns, common terms, the names of familiar objects. (Bernard was in the habit of saying that he found nothing nominal here; it was as real and literal and concrete as anything he had ever come across.) Like other aphasics of this kind, George was otherwise fluent and accurate and responded normally to others' speech. His fluency was especially notable; he was very good at not pausing at moments when a sympathetic hearer could have supplied the elusive word. Doctors, including Dr Mainwaring, had stated that the defect might clear up altogether in time, or might diminish to a greater or lesser extent in time, or might stay as it was, and that there was nothing to be done about it.

Shorty, who had followed George's discourse without trouble, said in a voice about an octave below his usual light tenor, 'Him fella big chief. Him fella like de blondes and de booze. Him fella like chucking de weight about. Him fella—'

'Bananas,' said George, then went on in an accusatory tone, 'But it's an outrage. I mean, this sort of behaviour's quite intolerable. You're not going to tell me that that's how a responsible politician carries on.'

'No, I'm not,' said Bernard. 'Nobody is. We're all on your side. As regards this topic.'

'All for one and one for all,' said Shorty. 'Hey, that reminds me of something. Old Paul Robeson. Another blackie.' He began to sing, giving himself full production in the way of arm and head movements, eye-rolling and the like. 'And each for a-a-all, we stand or fa-a-all, and all for each, until we reach, the journey's end. Oh-oh oh-oh, oh-oh oh-oh, oh-oh oh-oh, oh oh-oh, oh oh—'

'Did you watch, you know, the thing on the switching it on last night?' asked George.

'The television. Yes, we did,' lied Bernard swiftly. 'All the evening.'

'In that case you missed a most fascinating programme on, ah – that gadget there.' George indicated the wireless set on a small round table to the left of his bed. 'A play about one of these . . . Some chaps had missed their, anyhow they all had to wait in this, er, and one of them had lost his thing you have to show when you leave a country, at least another chap had lifted his, um, where he kept the . . .'

George gave some account of the play he had listened to, introducing a number of chronological leaps backward and forward that had not featured in the actual production, while Shorty hummed the Paul Robeson song fairly quietly and Bernard, shifting his position every few seconds, stood and waited. Eventually George said,

'Well, I mustn't keep you. I know you've got things to do, Shorty. Trevor and Tracy coming and all that.'

'Every man jack will have to pull together,' said Bernard with a loose-lipped smile.

'We'll pop in again later, George,' said Shorty. 'Be seeing you.'

'Nice of you to come up.'

Left alone, George thought of Bernard. It had indeed been nice of the old boy to pay his visit, but George had a shrewd suspicion that Adela's influence had been at work, as always. She gave the orders and Bernard took the line of least resistance. As far as he could, in all matters not affecting the regiment, he had done the same with poor Vera while they had been together. A proper man would have run things differently, taken the decisions himself. But – what could never be said could still, surely, be thought – but Bernard was not a proper man. The facts had to be faced: he had only married Vera because a senior officer had better be married, even perhaps because there had been pressure or at least advice from above. And Vera had married him because he had asked her, because she was forty, because she was a foreigner (having been fifteen on arrival, she had never lost her Czech accent) in an England just then grown hostile to foreigners, because indeed the year was 1938, when all thoughts of returning to Pilsen must finally be abandoned; and also because she had been fond of him.

George's reflections became vaguer, less like acts of memory than the inattentive turning-through of a book read many times before. Seen like this, from this distance, the wedding and the scandal had the look almost of a single event – the revelation that Bernard was having an affair with his servant, a Pte D. Shortell, the arrangement whereby Bernard had been allowed to send in his papers, to resign and salve the honour of the regiment instead of being cashiered, Vera's first departure, her return to find Bernard no longer interested in keeping up what had always been a pretence, her second and final departure. But there must have been some interval, if only because Vera had borne a child, a son who had emigrated to Canada at the earliest opportunity and never been heard of since.

That son, that nephew, named Stanley some way after his maternal grandfather, Stanislas, was never mentioned either. George half opened his eyes. He himself, he felt certain, would not have allowed any child of his to fall out of mind like that. But there was no such child; his wife had apologized to him in her last hours for its non-existence. What had he said in return? He never could remember.

The slam of a car door woke him. His watch showed twelve-forty. Splendid: practically the whole morning gone, and Trevor and Tracy due very soon.

Five

The sitting-room at Tuppenny-hapenny Cottage was the least dark room in the house, with a couple of fair-sized leaded windows look-ing on to the back garden. And today, at least, it was not cold. A log fire was well alight in the iron grate-basket, hissing steadily and emit-ting equally steady jets of smoke in various directions, but quite red underneath.

There was too much furniture and too many ornaments, because too many people had refused to part with too many of their larger possessions on coming here to live, and because the box-room upstairs was small, with a leaky ceiling which a succession of men had failed to repair after a lot of trying, or a lot of behaviour that might have suggested to a not very inquisitive observer that they were trying. Only George was under-represented in the sitting-room, since his physical and moral position prevented him from insisting effectively, even to Adela, that the box-room was an unsuitable place for part of his library, protected by a tarpaulin though it was.

So here were Shorty's huge unrepairable cuckoo-clock, his gold-painted trolley with glass trays, his full-colour reproduction showing a windjammer in a heavy sea, his black upright piano, which he played now and then on evenings when he was not too drunk to do so and Adela had not had a hard day. Bernard had contributed a rocking-chair, a nest of rosewood tables, a tiled coffee-table, a large terrestrial globe on a papier-mâché stand, a Benares brass bowl in which people had put their visiting-cards at one time, a sort of idol and a massive glass-fronted mahogany bookcase which had stayed locked with its key lost for over a year without causing inconvenience. Two upright chairs with tapestry seats and backs, one much worn, the other looking almost new, an oak wine-cooler now full of Michaelmas daisies, a second nest of tables, a watercolour of Anne Hathaway's cottage and a print of *Susanna and the Elders* belonged to Adela. There was in addition a gilt Louis Quinze suite comprising a sofa and two chairs, a Chippendale looking-glass and a half-life-size alabaster statuette of a nearly nude youth with his finger to his lips – a mute recommendation which, according to Bernard, was far too little heeded. These objects stood on a dark-red carpet bought second-hand in Newmarket, or hung on walls papered in a pattern of immense unidentified flowers and here and there exuding moisture.

One article owned in common was the radio. Bernard was listening to it now, or sat nearby while there issued from it, slightly off frequency, a short play about putatively comic clergymen. Within his reach stood a glass of tonic-water. It was not that he liked tonic-water much, just that, on advice that he would be dead in a few months if he went on as he was going, he had long given up alcohol, a step he sometimes pondered over. He was smoking a cigarette, not that he liked cigarettes much, just that smoking and not drinking seemed to him in some way better than not smoking and not drinking.

The door opened suddenly, with a thudding noise because it was considerably warped, and in came Marigold Pyke, the fifth of the five members of the household. She was seventy-three and, like Shorty, thought she could pass for sixty; in fact, she looked a very, very well-preserved seventy-three, with short white hair carefully blonde-rinsed, a figure still recognizably female, bright grey eyes, a lined mouth. Today she was dressed to kill, to annihilate utterly, thought Bernard as, not without reluctance, he glanced at her: trouser-suit in biscuit-coloured wool, frilly chiffon shirt, two-tone leather-and-suède shoes with tassels at the ends of the laces. Also in evidence were a handbag in worn but real crocodile-skin, its reality seldom left to be taken for granted, a jewelled brooch in the form of a miniature basket of flowers, a pair of unnaturally large pearl earrings, and a shagreen cigarette-holder attached by way of a corkscrew pin to a shagreen ring on the middle finger of the left hand. As always on viewing the last item afresh, Bernard was struck by the marvellously consistent high level of the rage it aroused in him, and his imagination filled with vague but inspiriting schemes for its disposal – mounting a fake burglary, contriving to slam the lid of Shorty's piano on it and the hand that wore it, etc.

'Good morning, Bernard.' Marigold's voice was of the sort that set minds like Bernard's in quest of wine-merchants' adjectives: round, full, fruity, well-matured, big. 'Any sign of Trevor and Tracy?' – her elder grandson and his wife.

'No sign I've been able to interpret as such, but then I don't know anything to speak of about divination. I certainly haven't noticed any comets or eclipses. On a more mundane level, if any sort of herald person had come prancing up to the door I'm pretty certain I should have been told, and quickly at that. Shorty's been about all the morning and I'm prepared to swear he wouldn't have kept anything like that from me.'

Marigold had, to put the action perhaps too prosaically, sat down on the Louis Quinze sofa, her property, like the glass and the silence-enjoining youth. 'Why do you dislike them so much? They're always nice to you.'

'Indeed they are, and I appreciate it, and I assure you I dislike them as little as I dislike anybody, less than most, in fact.'

'I think people in general would say that they're an exceptionally pleasant couple.'

'I've no doubt that, if challenged, people would say that.'

'Must we have that on?'

Bernard turned off the clergymen. There was silence, but not for long: Marigold felt she had not yet squarely made her point. She said,

'You wouldn't find a more agreeable pair of youngsters anywhere.'

'That may well be literally true.'

'They certainly are Mr and Mrs Trackle-Packles.'

This last expression, meaning roughly that the two under discussion were unusually attractive, was one of a large and extensible number habitually on Marigold's lips. And not only there: she had once had a checkle-peckle returned by her bank because it had been made out for five poundies. At the start, more than fifty years ago, she had used such phrases to gain what was planned as favourable social/sexual attention; later, their object had been simply to establish her as different from her contemporaries; nowadays, they turned up out of nothing more than force of habit, not consciously intended by her, barely noticed by those who had known her any length of time.

Even Bernard, at that moment, felt only a mild quickening of hostility. But he decided that, for one morning, he had put up with enough urging of what he was, or gave an appearance of being, already prepared to grant, and threw in a conversation-stopper of his most reliable sort. 'Trevor especially. Such fine hands.' (In fact he had never noticed Trevor's hands, would have been reluctant to state on oath that he was quite sure Trevor had hands, had for many years paid no attention to things like the hands of a young man, nice, pleasant, trackle-packles or other.)

The response was not only further silence, but a perceptible toss of the blondified head and a slow-motion fitting of a cigarette into the shagreen holder. 'Is there such a thing as a drink?'

'I'm afraid not. Haven't you heard? Drinks have ceased to exist. The Prime Minister made an announcement to that effect over the wireless just before you came in.'

Marigold laughed, thereby annoying Bernard, who had underestimated the amiability kindled in her by the impending visit. 'Could I possibly have one, do you think?'

'Very well, yes, I do. It must be possible, surely.'

For anything up to half a minute, Marigold looked over at the small array of bottles standing on one of the nests of tables, and, even without her spectacles as she was, might easily have been able to make out the South African sherry, the British vermouth, the Tunisian red wine, the Italian wine apéritif – a good buy, this last, relatively expensive but so vile that even Shorty could not get through a glass of it in much under the hour.

'Something *simple*,' said Marigold eventually.

'All those look quite straightforward to me.'

'No . . . I think . . . a small glass of that frightfully nice white wine

Adela sweetly gave me for my birthday. Would that be too much trouble? Just *half* a glass, Bernard.'

'Oh, just *half* a glass. That eases matters no end.'

Although Bernard's leg was really hurting that day, it was not hurting as much as his mode of rising from his chair suggested. Marigold, however, her face low over her opened handbag, appeared not to notice, whereupon he let a long wailing fart. She noticed that.

'You might have had the common courtesy to wait until you were out of the room.'

'I might well, yes, and I did try, but you were so long deciding on your drink that the pressure became impossible to withstand.'

'You ought to see a doctor.'

'Probably. Anyway, I've arranged to do so next week.'

Six

In the kitchen, Adela and Shorty were getting near the end of those preparations which could be made before the expected guests arrived: the sprouts were cooked and drained, the potatoes boiled and mashed with butter, or rather with the mixture of margarine and butter that Adela thought tasted just like butter, the consommé, already enriched with Cyprus cream sherry, was warming on the range. All that really remained was to take the foil off the roasting capon and put it higher in the gas-oven.

'I hope they're coming,' said Adela, for the third time in the last ten minutes.

'They'd have phoned else,' said Shorty from the stove. 'And they're not what you'd call late yet.'

'Because it would be such a waste, a waste of food, if they didn't, and such a disappointment.'

'There'd be no waste of food, I promise you.'

'But it would still be a disappointment. Marigold's been looking forward to it for days and days.'

'I must say I do think it wouldn't be out of turn for her to be lending a bit of a hand, Adela. It's her kid, or her kid's kid, rather.'

'You know how she is, not knowing where to find anything so that it's quicker for us to do it ourselves. Not that she's the only one.'

For Bernard now stood between them, looking slightly helpless. After so many years, slightly helpless was as helpless as he needed to look in order to convey his point to the other two.

'Kin I elp yer wiv anyfink, squire?' asked Shorty. 'Render yer hassistance, like, eh, swelp me?'

'Marigold wants that wine of hers. I was wondering where the—'

'Say no more. The capable Shorty will handle the problem, on the understanding that you take over here for a minute, pursuing your duty with zeal and conscientiousness. I can't see it bothering your leg, but correct me if I'm wrong.'

Bernard began stirring the indicated pan of bread sauce, to him a demeaning chore but substantially preferable to the alternative, while Shorty, lurching slightly with drink, went off to the coal-house, a commodious structure cold enough at almost any season to act as a cellar.

'I got you the *Telegraph*,' said Adela.

'Thank you. Where is it? I'm supposed to keep—'

'Oh, all right. Here.'

With a nod of further thanks, Bernard took the newspaper, but did not then and there make a start on its front page, as he would once have done. These days it and its contemporaries seemed like parish magazines of another parish than his own. He would none the less spend a large part of the afternoon reading it.

'I do wish they'd come,' said Adela.

'So do I.'

'There wasn't as much traffic as I'd expected. And what do you think? – a very nice young boy, he couldn't have been more than about twenty, he carried the groceries to the car. Just picked up the box; I didn't have to ask him. I gave him ten p and he smiled so sweetly. I think a lot of them are like that really; it's just that they're so different in other ways.'

'I don't think they're much different.'

'Well, that is strange, coming from you, Bernard. You must be mellowing in your old age.'

Bernard managed to say nothing to that. He stirred away with more vigour. Why, he wondered, did he consciously want to upset his sister's innocent satisfaction, throw cold water on her mild pleasure at having found her expedition that little bit less taxing than she had feared? Why was it out of the question for him to produce some banal but acceptable Shorty-style phrase about a stroke of luck or people not being as black as they were painted? Because, today or yesterday or longer ago, he had stopped bothering to pretend to himself that he was different from what he had always been.

While they talked, and now after they had fallen silent, Adela had got on with laying the table. All meals, except George's, were eaten here in the kitchen, because what had been the dining-room was now Marigold's bedroom. George obviously had to be on the same floor as the bathroom; there were only three conceivable bedrooms on that first floor, one shared by Bernard and Shorty, another occupied by Adela, the latter draughty, facing north, altogether less attractive than the former dining-room, and in general unsuitable for an invalid. So it had been Marigold who, with remarkably little fuss, had agreed to move downstairs on George's arrival.

In a moment, Shorty reappeared with a bottle of the bad-year Muscadet that Adela had picked up cheap at the off-licence, and made straight, or reasonably straight, for the dresser drawer in which for nine years he had kept the corkscrew, an instrument whose whereabouts he permanently needed to know. His hand was reaching for the drawer in question when Adela said,

'Corkscrew in the left-hand dresser drawer, Shorty.'

'Oh, thanks, Adela.'

Bernard said nothing to that either. He watched Shorty uncork and pour. Then Adela looked up from her nearly-completed task with a sudden smile.

'Here they are. You can turn that down and leave it, Bernard.'

She ran out of the kitchen like a rugby forward following up a kick. It was clear that Shorty too had heard sounds of arrival, but, possibly mindful of his vestigial place as a servant, he made no move to go and welcome the guests. Bernard, not having heard, followed his sister at a less headlong pace. By a calculated omission, he left Marigold's simple drink behind.

Seven

Trevor Fishwick, Marigold's daughter's son, stood on the cracked stone doorstep of Tuppenny-hapenny Cottage and swung the wrought-iron knocker. Rust or corrosion impeded its movement; it gave a feeble tap that must have been inaudible indoors, even to normal hearing. But no further attempt was needed: muffled footfalls could be heard fast approaching, and a very female voice raised. Before the door was thrown open, Trevor squeezed his wife's hand.

In a moment he was in his grandmother's embrace, being kissed with little tense groaning noises that Shorty had once compared to those of somebody straining on the bog. Released after an interval, Trevor moved on to Adela, gripped her by the upper arms to forestall any attempt at a hug, and kissed her briefly. Tracy, coached in advance, did the same when it came to her turn. She would have done more if Adela had not smelt so old.

Bernard had hung back. He had glimpsed the Fishwicks' car while the door was open and felt wrath stirring. All cars displeased him, and not just for superficial reasons like the noise they made or their tendency to be painted bright colours. They were like horses as seen by a foot soldier: damned nuisances, much too much fuss made about them, needing constant attention, ridiculous that grown men should be reduced to depending on them. This particular car was outstandingly objectionable. It was larger and newer than the one he had at any rate a financial stake in; far more galling, it belonged to someone of twenty-five or thirty or whatever it was. The youngster seemed to think he had a perfect right to buy it and stuff it with petrol and oil and drive it about all over the place just as he felt inclined. And did he have to have all that hair growing from his head and face, outwards from his face, a good deal of it *forwards* from his face? It was extraordinary, and also typical, that he apparently had quite a responsible job in something he chose to call electrics, or perhaps electronics.

'Good of you to come all this way, my boy,' said Bernard, dealing out one of the soft lateral handshakes Trevor so much disliked.

'Only from Cambridge, actually. I had this business call to make there.'

'Oh yes, of course. Still . . .'

Bernard limped over and made a kissing movement in the direction of Tracy's cheek.

'Come along, darlings, and have a drinkle-pinkle,' cried Marigold, putting unusual animation into the idionym. When she added, 'You must be simply frozen,' both Bernard and Trevor, unknown to each other, silently mouthed the phrase in time with her.

In the sitting-room, which was almost warm by now and not very smoky, Trevor took from a plastic carrier-bag the three bottles he had chosen with some care at a cash-and-carry store: a pricey Chablis for his grandmother, a dry Spanish sherry so that Adela and Tracy and he could drink something they liked, and a cognac as a collective gift. The older women said it was sweet of him but he really should not have done it. Shorty was summoned to act as barman, then at once departed again to fetch the corkscrew, and incidentally, on a safe reckoning, to put down the glass of Muscadet poured just now for Marigold. Having returned and got a drink into everyone's hand except Bernard's, he joined the party.

Over the years, Trevor had grown used to this move at such a time, but it still aroused in Tracy a feeling that seldom visited her: embarrassment. She would have claimed vigorously that she was not a snob; nevertheless she was disconcerted, made not to know what to say or where to look, when chatted to and Christian-named by somebody who had been behaving like a servant a couple of minutes before and who would, she knew from previous visits, do more of the same at the lunch-table. The servant-like behaviour was not just a matter of doing servant-like tasks, it was doing them in a servant-like way, with a servant's expression, movements, carriage; perhaps being an actress helped one to see these things. And – she would again have denied that she had anything against pooves – there was the boyfriend angle. The trouble with it was nothing so specific as imagining these two old men messing about with each other: Bernard, at least, must have been past it for years and years. No, it was just that, whereas meeting a man and his wife did not by any means necessarily bring up the idea of sex, meeting a pair of pooves of any age necessarily did, and these two were old, and the idea of sex in any relation to the old, any relation at all, was obscene. It was a great pity, but there it was. Tracy had heard people talk as if admiringly of old So-and-so who was still fucking like a stoat at over seventy; it was only talk, with no thought behind it.

Trevor had been telling his grandmother, on urgent request, about the work he had been doing recently. He simplified everything as much as he could short of downright falsification, a vain scruple, he knew, for the simplified version was still about as difficult for somebody like her as, say, fast colloquial French in a strong Norman accent, or would have been were she listening. He understood quite well that she was acting on two related principles: that men liked talking about their work and that it was important, especially for an old lady, to seem interested, or to keep quiet, while they did so. The whole thing was a game, but it had to be played out as conscientiously as possible.

'Of course,' ended Trevor, 'the control has to ignore changes due to the weather and heating and so on and only take notice of readings that suggest a fire's broken out.'

'How fascinating, Trevor dear. You are so terribly lucky to be so clever and have a job you *enjoy* so much.' Conscientious on her own part, Marigold turned to Tracy, whom she genuinely liked and approved of, envied no more than was reasonable, and would have considered quite pretty in a tall dark pale way if the girl had ever taken any trouble with her appearance. 'And what about you, darling? I saw you in that Strindberg thing, we all did, and thought you were simply marvellous.'

'Very natural, Tracy,' said Shorty. 'Very natural.'

'Thank you. Well, I go into rehearsal next week for another of the Professor Pobble series. I play the scientist who's trying to get him.'

'Kids' show, that, isn't it?'

Unlike her granddaughter-in-law, Marigold had a vast amount more than nothing against what in her terminology were nancy-boys, active and superannuated alike. Among the many other groups she had a similar quantity against were lower-class persons, lower-class persons who had come the smallest distance up in the world (this lower-class person had done well enough in a minor way of business to buy himself a still fully adequate annuity, was in fact subsidizing her to some extent, so he qualified with honours), and drunks. Altogether, then, it was with some emphasis that she now said to Shorty,

'That is neither here nor there. An actress has to learn to play in any type of production if she's a professional like Tracy. Damn it, I ought to know.'

Not more than a pinch of shit you oughtn't, said Shorty to himself, having heard enough from Adela to conclude that Marigold's very often mentioned stage career had been undistinguished and brief. But he was better at hiding his feelings than some of his housemates, and all he said aloud was,

'Oh, I appreciate that, Marigold. I was just making sure I'd got the right programme. It's good – I quite often watch it.'

'You know nothing whatever about these things.'

'Is this in the West End?' asked Adela.

'Further west than that, I fancy,' said Bernard. 'At or near Shepherd's Bush, if I remember rightly.'

'I didn't know there was a theatre there.'

'There may or may not be. I was referring to the BBC television centre.'

'How do you know that?'

'Is it a closely-guarded secret?'

'But you never look at the television.'

'Nevertheless the information has reached me somehow.'

'Actually it's Medway TV,' said Tracy. 'In Baker Street.'

'Oh,' said Bernard with an air of distaste.

'You see,' said Adela.

'I see? What do I see? How do I see? See?'

'What's your news, Goldie?' asked Trevor, using the diminutive Marigold had decreed upon her grandchildren.

'You don't want to listen to an old woman's gossip.'

'Just who you've heard from, that sort of thing,' said Trevor with commendable speed.

'Now which of my chummy-wummies would you remember? . . . What about Jill Grigson-Morse? She used to come to us in Beauchamp Place.'

Trevor's face seemed to light up. 'Oh, yes.'

'No, you couldn't have seen her there, because she didn't come back from Italy until after we'd left Beauchamp Place. Her husband had a job in the Diplomatic, I think, or . . .'

'How's he getting on?'

'Oh, he died it must be ten years ago. A very slow and painful cancer. She was absolutely marvellous all the way to the end. She's a brave woman.'

'How is she these days?'

'I was just coming to that. I had a letter from her yesterday or the day before. They've had to take her other leg off, but she's awfully good about it. I do so admire people like that.'

At least the poor bitch didn't have her bloody leggle-peggle whipped off, thought Shorty, saying, 'That glass is looking pretty sick, Marigold. Here, let me top it up for you. There we are. Funny, I've never really taken to white wine, ever. Too sharp, somehow. Tastes do differ, don't they? Tracy, you're on the sherry.'

'No more for me, thank you. No, yes, I will, please.'

'But I heard from Emily Rouse just this morning. She's much better, poor thing. She can get up and sit in a chair most days now. You remember her, of course, Trevor dear.'

'I think so, yes.' Trevor told himself it was all physiological, all bodily chemistry, not a thing they or anybody else could do about it.

'She was a great beauty in the Twenties. One of the Bright Young Things, as they used to call them then; always having her picture in the papers. There was a certain very famous person who died only a year or two ago who was quite devoted to her. Oh, literally hundreds of men were always pestering her to marry them, but she never would, and now she's—'

'How's George?' asked Trevor.

'George?'

'Professor George Zeyer, possibly,' said Bernard. 'Of this address.'

'Oh, he's had a stroke,' said Adela – 'not another one, I mean, but he had that stroke, so he can't move about much. Still can't move about much. Well, at all. Not really.'

'Let's get him down here.'

'I don't really think—' began Bernard.

'Good idea, Trevor,' said Shorty with animation. 'Spiffing suggestion, actually, old fruit.'

'But he can't walk.'

'Trevor and I'll carry him, Adela. Hoots, he's nae more nor a wee laddie is yon.'

Eight

George sat in bed with that month's issue of a learned journal open in front of him. At least he was trying to keep it open, but with only his wrong hand available he could not weaken its spine enough to make it lie flat, and the pages constantly closed and closed again and had him fumbling for his place with that wrong hand. In fact the journal held no more than half his attention; the sound of voices from downstairs came readily to his unimpaired hearing, Marigold's voice more than others'. Well, it was her day. Luncheon-time must be near: it looked, then, as if he would get his ten minutes of Trevor and Tracy before they had to be off back to London, rather than before they had to be off down to luncheon. On the whole, that would be preferable, because it would break up the interval before luncheon and tea. No, here they came now, or here came somebody, two people if not more.

Two it was. Trevor and Shorty entered the bedroom and Trevor gave him a warm left-handed handshake as he had done before.

'Hallo, George old chap: how's things?'

'Shut up, you,' said George, but he said it to Mr Pastry, who was growling tremulously. Then he said, 'I'm fine, Trevor, thanks. How nice of you to come up. You're looking—'

Shorty had taken the plaid dressing-gown from its hook behind the door. 'Right, George, you're on your way to join the party.'

'Oh, you don't want me; besides, I'm—'

'Oh yes we do, me old cock-sparrer. Just you slip into this and we'll have you down there in two shakes of a lamb's tail, not to speak of other appurtenances such as one might or might not possess.'

While the other two got him into his dressing-gown, George felt a physical thrill of excitement such as he had not felt for a long time, much longer than the months he had spent under this roof. All he had ever seen of the ground floor had been those parts which a man half carried straight upstairs from the front door could have expected to see. Now everything was changed: if he could be moved about like this on one occasion, then, given the presence of a second able-bodied man to assist Shorty, the same thing could happen on many, perhaps every couple of weeks or so. A precedent was being set. George wondered a little what Bernard thought of the present manoeuvre; but, whatever anyone might think, that manoeuvre was now in train. As the first excitement ebbed, hope replaced it.

'You're so kind, both of you,' said George at the top of the stairs. 'You don't know what this means to me. I shall never forget it.'

Nine

At the foot of the stairs, Bernard stood and watched the descent of the trio. He was there from a mixture of motives. First was the hope that Shorty might be drunk enough to drop George or even bring the three of them pitching down the stairs. That would go some way to compensate for his own failure just now to block the operation under way; it was no comfort to protest to himself that he had never had a fair chance, that George's two helpers had reached their joint decision in a flash and gone to execute it with the speed of promotion-hungry firemen. Secondly, to watch so closely and obviously would embarrass George and might also, thirdly, be mistaken by Adela for sympathetic concern. But what of that? What if she saw her brother's interest as it was? Habit must be at work, the habit of wanting to be mistaken for a man of ordinary decent feeling.

George's impending presence meant that it had been a total, as opposed to a nearly total, waste of time to do him earlier, true, but this loss was more than offset by the likely effect on others. The length, even the bare fact, of his conversational intrusions could not fail to annoy Marigold, and their style might well disconcert the two young people, if anything ever could.

When the party had half a dozen stairs still to go, Pusscat, Marigold's spayed tortoiseshell, arrived on the scene, recognized Bernard and, as always on doing so, hurriedly left the scene again by the nearest exit. This happened to be up the staircase. Pusscat passed between Trevor and the wall without trouble and disappeared from view, only to reappear almost at once pursued by Mr Pastry, who, evidently alive by now to there being some novelty afoot, had wandered out on to the landing. Cat and dog reached the descending three within the same second. There were lurches, stumbles, cries, but George, held fast by Trevor, stayed relatively upright, and it was Shorty who fell – not far or badly, however, his head missing by almost a yard the large brass-bound basket that, full of sodden logs, stood near the sitting-room doorway.

Bernard held out a hand to Shorty, who got up unaided. The animals were nowhere to be seen.

'That damned dog,' said Bernard with real feeling.

'Not his fault,' said Shorty. 'No harm done.'

'It's his nature to chase a, you know, tabby one when he sees one,' said George.

'Now let's think.' Bernard had had time to do so. 'I suggest we take George straight out to the kitchen. Luncheon must be just about ready and we don't want to get him settled in there and have to move him all over again in a couple of minutes.'

Shorty guessed that this proposed arrangement was intended to make George feel he was due for less of a party than he might have been expecting, but said nothing.

'I don't want to be a nuisance to anyone,' said George.

Ten

It was, in fact, a quarter of an hour later that the five residents and two guests were gathered in the kitchen. Under the low ceiling, the bare table, laid as it was, had an unfestive look. It was bare because Adela and Shorty were always spilling things, which weighed against the use of a linen cloth, and the susceptibilities of Marigold and Bernard, in accord for once, ruled out any sort of plastic one. Shorty, of course, would have settled for a few thicknesses of newspaper.

Marigold, flanked by her grandson and his wife, sat opposite George, Bernard at the head. Adela served the consommé, Shorty offered a choice of beer, stout and cider. By Adela's decree, wine was only provided at Christmas and birthday parties; the rest of the time, they could not afford enough of anything worth drinking, enough, that is, to satisfy Shorty and not let the rest of the company have to scramble for a second glass.

'What a happy day,' said Marigold. 'It's so nice to have some young people in the house. Especially, if I may say so, these young people.'

'You may say so,' said Bernard, stressing all four words equally.

'It makes one forget one's old and on the scrap-heap.'

'Drives it completely out of one's mind. As if one had never entertained the thought.'

'It's a marvellous treat for me,' said George. 'Just to be sitting at this, er, sitting here and joining in and having a, something to drink with all of you instead of eating off, uh, upstairs. Do you know, this is the very first time I've ever been in this room? Oh, I'm not complaining; it's obviously very—'

'I can promise you it won't be the last, George.' Adela was still suffering from the most acute self-reproach for never having seriously considered the simple procedure gone through today by Trevor and Shorty. It was no excuse to say that routines were easily fallen into, that old age cramped the imagination. She must make a real effort to think of others for a change.

'If it weren't for this bloody leg of mine,' said Bernard, 'we could manage it every day.'

'I'm sure I could do it if I tried,' said Adela.

'Coming down you probably could, Adela,' said Shorty. 'Going up's a different share of pooze.'

'A different what?'

'Sorry, spoonerizing again. A different pair of shoes. Different. It'd be different taking George upstairs again. Different to bringing him down.'

Adela's expression cleared at last. 'Harder, you mean. Yes, I can see how it would be.' She was not being sarcastic, just making sure that Shorty knew he had been understood, as she herself had always liked to know she had been understood. 'We'll have a go at it before Trevor leaves. So that if it's too much for me we can still get George back to his room – you and Trevor can.'

'Ah, I think I have it,' said Bernard, frowning in pretended concentration.

'Have it?'

Marigold began to speak while Bernard was still inhaling deeply. 'When are you two young ones going to start producing some kiddle-widdles?'

'It's a question of money, really,' said Trevor after a moment. He set about accumulating the will to explain yet once more that, with his full approval, Tracy was determined to pursue her acting career, that an infant Fishwick would therefore have to have some sort of proper nursemaid, that any sort of proper nursemaid would have to have a whole series of things that also cost money; but he need not have bothered.

'Oh, money, money, money,' cried his grandmother. 'I know we live in a materialistic society, but I'd have expected you of all people to be able to rise above that. How many poundies is a baby worth?'

'The patter of tiny feet,' said Shorty, pouring himself more stout. 'Il belleeesimo bambeeeno. Sure-a, what's a home-a without-a the little-a ones-a?'

'It isn't just, just money, Goldie,' said Tracy. 'If I'm going to—'

'Children aren't a luxury, they're a necessity.' Marigold was off now, as all her hearers had been waiting for her to be: off, that is, not in any expected or unexpected direction, just somewhere. 'You may think I'm a sentimental old fool. Oh, no – severely practical, I assure you. Where should I be now without my children and my children's children? Answer me that.'

Among others, Trevor would have liked to do so. His answer would have mentioned two or three rather nasty places in any one of which he thought the old girl should be now instead of where she was, lauding parenthood in this company. A remarkably comprehensive as well as roughly uniform company it was, now he came to flip through it in his mind: apart from the as yet childless couple just now under discussion of a sort, who he knew could end that state any time they fancied, there were present one person altogether uninterested in what had to be done in order to produce children, one who could never have had a chance of bearing a child, one who had very likely tried to beget a child but had failed, and one whose single child might in effect never have existed. It was only thoughtlessness, tactlessness, Trevor told himself charitably, not malice, a motive that demanded genuine and close interest in other people.

In fact, Marigold had seen quite early that her tirade might be hurtful to Bernard if he was listening, and, in the hope that it was and he was, prolonged it until Adela and Shorty had served the main course. (To be fair, the risk of also hurting Adela did not cross Marigold's mind.) Then, wanting to talk about an old friend who was not only childless but unmarried, who in due course turned out – rather to Trevor's surprise – to be still mobile, and whom incidentally none of the others present had ever met, she put in a brief transition passage about some people's ability to manage without children, thus absently throwing away what there had been of her argument, and was off again.

'. . . I've never known such energy. That woman is a human dynamo. Of course, she's slowed down a little in the last few years. To my certain knowledge she hasn't had more than, yes, two, no, three holidays since she started work.'

'I met a girl from New Zealand a little while ago,' said Tracy just as an outsize forkful of capon was entering Marigold's mouth. 'She told me—'

The intervention was fractionally too soon. Marigold snatched the forkful out again and said, 'She says she can't see any reason for them in her case. Why should she stop doing what she most enjoys doing just because everybody else goes dashing off to the south of France or Italy for three weeks every year? I must say I see her point.'

Tracy did not want to have it thought, even by someone like Shorty, that she considered her having met a girl from New Zealand a little while ago to be in itself a worthwhile offering. She waited until Marigold had started chewing before she said, 'This New Zealand girl—'

She was fractionally too late: Marigold did a mighty swallow. 'And the holidays she did have weren't really holidays. She'd been going at things too hard and was ordered to drop everything and have a rest. Her dockle-pockles said they wouldn't be responsible if she didn't.'

'It can't have been much fun for her family,' said Adela into a silence.

'How do you mean?'

'Well . . . either they must have gone away without her or not have had any holidays either.'

'She hasn't got any family. She's always been single.'

'Oh, I thought you were talking about people having children.'

'I was, but that was hours ago.'

'Oh, I thought you still were.'

'I distinctly told you she was single.'

'I'm sorry, I must have missed that.'

'You must,' said Bernard jocularly. 'Indeed you must. It was necessary so that you could yet again get hold of the wrong end of the stick through the eye of a needle in a haystack.'

'I'm sorry,' said Adela again. She felt breathless for a moment and put it down to the strain of organizing the lunch-party on top of the supermarket expedition, the excitement of having visitors. 'I didn't do it on purpose; it's just that until almost this moment I've had this rather essential job on my hands, do you see.'

Bernard showed mild perplexity. 'What was that?'

'I said I was sorry I got mixed up, but I've had a lot to think about.'

'I heard every word you said. My tone might have told you that the "that" I was inquiring about referred not to your remark in its entirety but to something mentioned in it. What, in fact, was your "rather essential job"?'

'Oh, honestly . . . Shopping and cooking and seeing to all the—'

'I *see*,' said Bernard, in wonder and yet in ready acceptance.

There was another brief silence. Tracy did not break it. Now in the apparent position of being obsessed with the New Zealand girl, she would not run the risk of seeming clinically insane on the subject. Trevor glanced at her with sympathy, with affection too: after a session like this, a lot of wives would give their husbands a stupendous ballocking as soon as they were alone, but this wife never did anything of that sort, never would in fifty years. Or might people have said the same of Marigold when she was twenty-three? Very few people; surely to God, very few indeed.

'Christmas, darlings,' said Marigold. 'Christmas. Do please say you really are coming – I couldn't face it without you. Not *begin* to.'

Trevor said sturdily, 'All fixed, Goldie. We'll be here in good time for lunch, and not off again till late, the later the better, in a way. I mean it'll be easier driving. Because the roads'll be clearer. Less traffic.'

'And Rachel and . . . and Keith? The last cardie I had, she said they weren't absolutely certain they could get away. Have you heard anything?'

'Yes, they're coming too.'

'On Boxing Day.'

'They can't make Boxing Day. They'll be down with us.'

Rachel, Trevor's cousin, and her husband Keith, apart from the Fishwicks the only connections of Marigold's not under a vow of never again entering Tuppenny-hapenny Cottage, had told Trevor with unsurpassable emphasis that it was going to be Christmas Day or nothing, with the rider that, should either or both of the Fishwicks happen to walk under a bus on Christmas Eve, it was going to be nothing, or, to quote Keith on the point, fucking fuck-all.

Marigold hid her disappointment. 'It'll be so wonderful to have the four of you here. Quite divine.'

At the last word, Bernard's shoulders jerked slightly. He knew, knew as certainly as that the sun would rise in the morning, that she had come across it in some terrifying book on the manners and customs of the Twenties, the decade she believed herself to have notably adorned. He did not speak.

George did. He had some idea that he might bore people thereby, but considered the risk more worth taking than that of giving an impression, by prolonged silence, of failure to enjoy himself. 'Well, it's the children's time, isn't it? I know nobody'll be actually blowing up, ah, coloured things you hang up, and I don't suppose there'll be any, you stretch them from one corner of the, er, one corner to the other, but we'll have, you write things down games, and we'll have . . . prickly green stuff and Christmas, uh, thing you eat at the end of the meal, you set it alight, and all the, people send them and they'll be on the, um . . .'

'On the fifth day of Christmas my true-love sent to me,' sang Shorty, 'five go-old rings, four calling birds, three French hens, two—'

Bernard's hand came down fairly hard on the table. 'Before the top of my head comes flying off and starts circling round the room, could we have quiet for, say, ten seconds?'

The tone of his voice matched the style in which he had put his request, but, to Trevor, his look did not. Bernard's genial expressions of irritation and suave snubs were familiar enough and to spare, but this was anger, or hatred. For a moment, Trevor felt disquiet, before he remembered that in half an hour or so Tracy and he could decently be out of the place.

Eleven

The Fishwicks had departed and George was back in his bed, but he was not as he had been before their arrival: listless, overborne by his handicaps, concerned only with getting through the day. Now, his mind was full of schemes and prospects.

To deal with the most obvious point first – it had not escaped him that, behind that urbane exterior, Bernard was a moody old customer, and his occasional mild outbursts must not be taken too seriously. All the same, the display of annoyance he had given at the luncheon-table had been, in part, justifiably provoked. That senile drivel about blowing up, oh, what the hell were they called? – *balloons*, and Christmas . . . pudding – with a real effort one could get it almost straight away – would have tried the patience of a saint. In his new condition George could see such things quite clearly, and apologized in his thoughts for having been the source of so much vexation over the past months.

But that was not to the purpose; it was time gone by. The idea now was to work as hard as possible to prevent any such exhibition in the future. He spoke three languages without accent and could read four others; surely it was not beyond him, even at his age, to learn what was in effect an eighth tongue, a form of English that avoided those damnable common nouns. Even a cumbersome periphrasis, *provided it were delivered at normal conversational speed*, would be far preferable to the halting, fragmentary, er-and-um style he had let himself drift into. And it would take no great effort to arrive at the shortest intelligible periphrasis for any given object and simply memorize it, just as one memorized idioms and sayings when learning a conventional language. The task could be split up into sections like those of an elementary phrase-book: In the Bedroom, At the Tea-Table, In the Garden – yes, after today, even that might be possible when the warmer weather came. Half an hour every morning, and every afternoon – perhaps longer: he would see how it went – devising and practising the special vocabulary.

More than that, much more than that, he was going to start work again. His intelligence and, such matters as balloons and Christmas puddings apart, his memory were unimpaired. The basic parts of his library were still to hand – if not immediately to hand, at any rate not beyond access, given some co-operation on Shorty's or Adela's part. He could sell his old desk typewriter, which weighed a ton, and get a light plastic model he could have on his lap and operate easily enough, however slowly. The journals and book pages were becoming more and more prone to the grossest errors of pure fact, not to speak of interpretations that could be called eccentric at best. That very morning he had come across yet another repetition of the lie that Mihailović had collaborated with the Germans. Three books and a number of articles had made George Zeyer's name sufficiently well known in his field. A letter to the editor over that name would carry weight; after a couple of weeks' interval, a different sort of letter, one asking for books to review or suggesting a contribution on some current question at issue, might well bring a favourable response. Anyhow, he was going to have a try.

And further yet . . . he was no longer truly bedridden, bedbound. No matter how seldom, he would be downstairs, and there would be the garden possibility, and even a car-journey to Newmarket (a place as enticing as Paris or Venice had been in years gone by) was not to be ruled out. One occasion was a certainty, Christmas Day: he could trust Adela to see to that.

All these changes in his situation and outlook were the work of Shorty and Trevor. Which of them had thought of fetching him to the luncheon-party? Never mind: he would get the solicitor fellow along and draw up a new will, leaving each of them fifty pounds and the residue to Adela, instead of making Adela his sole beneficiary. She would understand; well, he would make sure she did. There was no need for hurry.

Exertion, and the two glasses of beer he had drunk, were making George drowsy. He could afford a little nap; paradoxically, having made plans to fill his time, he felt it was all right to let some of it go to waste. For the first time under this roof, he felt at home. The line of photographs on the chest of drawers – his wife, Vera, his departmental colleagues at the university, the university buildings – looked like part of the room, not forlorn mementoes ripped from their context.

Someone knocked at his door: Adela, in a state of mild distress. She came over to the bedside and blinked at him through her heavy glasses.

'Hallo, Adela dear.'

'George, I must apologize to you.'

'What on earth for?'

'Though I don't see how anybody could apologize enough. I've been so thoughtless all these months, letting you lie here day in day out and just never seeing how easy it is to get you up and down stairs.'

'It isn't easy at all. It was too much for you in the end, getting me up, and there's nobody else to give Shorty a hand.'

'I've been wrapped up in my own affairs.'

'You've got the whole house to run.'

'Another day I might be better. It had been rather a busy morning.'

'You're not to overstrain yourself.'

'We must work something out.'

'Don't worry about it.'

'It was so obvious all the time and I never thought of it.'

'That's enough. None of the rest of us would probably be alive if it weren't for you. You must know that.'

Adela would have liked to kiss George, but did not venture to; she gripped his hands in turn, starting with the wrong one.

'Off for your walk?'

'Just a few minutes: it'll be pretty wet. I'll be up with your tea at four-thirty.'

'Bless you, Adela.'

Twelve

Going down the stairs, Adela felt a small twinge of pain. Though not in quite the usual place, it must be her ulcer deploring the tensions of the last few hours and the two glasses of sherry she had taken before luncheon. It was the same every time they had visitors: her conviction that one drink was her limit, previously quite firm, would vanish in the bustle of conversation. She wished she had a particle of her brother's will-power – firmly on the bottle until (how long was it now?) ten years ago or more, a fortnight of steadily reduced intake, then not another drop. Presumably he had long since stopped missing it.

Now she knocked at Marigold's door, heard, as expected, a voice heavy with preoccupation, and went in. Also as expected, Marigold was hard at work. This afternoon it was her address-book she was hard at work on, but it might just as well have been her knitting-patterns, her screen with the coloured cutouts from newspapers and magazines, her wardrobes, her photograph-album, her correspondence, the objects on and in her dressing-table; these last were in constant need of rearrangement.

'Who is it?' she asked in the same tone; to see who it was she would have had to turn through an arc of nearly ninety degrees, and also raise her head.

'It's Adela, dear. I was wondering if you felt like a stroll. The rain seems to have—'

'Yes, I could do with a breath of fresh air. I'll just get my bootle-pootles on.'

This was unexpected. Normally, Marigold would conduct a full debate with herself, most though not all of it aloud, on the question whether or not to accompany Adela on her daily afternoon stroll, and when she agreed it would be with an air of concession. Now, she seemed almost eager.

If Adela had ever had a friend, it was Marigold. They had met at school in 1912. Their contemporaries there had often remarked on how nice (most of the time) Marigold was to Adela and how devoted (all the time) Adela was to Marigold. When Marigold's husband had his final and fatal heart-attack in 1969, leaving her what finally turned out to be a few hundred pounds, some furniture and nowhere to live, it had been obvious common sense to throw in her lot with Adela. Adela had the benefit of her company, and kept house too. Not many people, perhaps, could have put up with the constant presence of a couple as objectionable as Marigold found Bernard and Shorty, but Marigold managed it, with an ease that sometimes surprised her.

The two women, one protected against the mud and wet grasses by scarlet plastic boots, the other by wellingtons, left the cottage by the back door and made their way into the woods under a flat grey sky. Water dripped off trees and bushes, and there was an occasional beating of wings. Otherwise it was very quiet.

'I hope you enjoyed the party, dear,' said Adela.

'Oh yes, I thought it went off reasonably well, considering. I just wish your brother would learn to control his temper when we have guests. And Shorty was rolling drunk, of course.'

'Oh, I think Bernard was only being a bit sort of gruff. He's probably been having trouble with his, you know, disposal arrangements. And Shorty, well, he doesn't seem to realize that at his age he can't—'

'We all have our troubles, it's quite true, and we've just got to try not to be too hard on one another.'

This, coming from Marigold, might have struck a different observer as the very rough equivalent of an assertion by a Jew that Himmler had perhaps been judged too harshly, but Adela said no more than,

'Yes, tolerance is the great thing. Actually, Bernard's not too bad there, he can be not too bad sometimes. He was telling me only this morning he thought young people were much nicer than people say. Than a lot of older people say, I mean. It's only when he—'

'Darling, something rather silly happened today.'

'Oh yes? Tell me about it.'

Marigold did not at once respond to this encouragement. She and her companion came into a small clearing where there was moss, a tree-stump and a thick drift of dead leaves. Just then, Shorty was seen approaching. His course was far from straight, though it was true that his path bent to and fro among birch and ash trees and that he was pushing a wheelbarrow. He had used it to take a load of empty bottles, tin cans and the like to a large hole in the ground a couple of hundred yards away and dump it there, as he did every other day or so; a chore, and almost certainly illegal, but cheaper and more effective than trying to bribe the dustmen, who called only once a week, into removing the stuff, which must regularly have exceeded some unproclaimed quota.

'Hallo, girls,' said Shorty as he crossed to them. 'Look what I've got.'

What he had got, lying in the barrow, was a large hen pheasant, soaking wet but otherwise, to all appearance, in excellent condition. After some initial surprise, Adela responded to the sight with interest, Marigold with obvious discomfort.

'It was just lying by the path; can't have been dead long.'

'You can't tell,' said Adela. 'It might be a day or two.'

'But you hang them longer than that, don't you, Adela? I'm going to take it home and dry it off and string it up in the larder.'

Adela was dubious. 'Of course, we don't know how it died. It might have eaten poison. Put down by somebody. To kill vermin and things.'

'Unlikely, I'd say. You never see a soul in these woods.'

'I don't care how it died,' said Marigold violently, 'I'm not having anything to do with it.'

Frowning, she picked the bird up by its feet and threw it back-handed into the trees, where it thumped faintly to the ground and disappeared.

'Well, that takes care of that,' said Shorty. 'It was just a thought.' He had instantly grasped that Marigold's action was the result of genuine feeling, not of any desire to make an impression, and in the second place that that feeling was not caused simply by confrontation with a dead pheasant. He resolved to stay about for a while and see what more of the same there might be to come. 'Are you ladies proceeding further? If so, I request permission to accompany you, leaving my trusty barrow where it now stands.'

'If you don't *terribly* mind, Shorty,' said Marigold with hidden effort, 'there is something rather particular I wanted to say to Adela, so . . .'

'So I'll go rejoicing on my way. Thank you, thank you, thank you.'

When Shorty, just not quite falling over as he pushed the barrow out of the clearing, had left them, Marigold turned to Adela.

'As I said, darling, it is only a silly little thingle-pingle, but it has been sort of bothering me. You remember I mentioned that letter from Emily Rouse, where she said she was—'

'Oh, I can see how that might bother you, but you really ought to feel cheered up by the way she's improved. People can—'

'It isn't that, it isn't that. Would you kindly let me say what I have to say?'

'I'm sorry, dear.'

Marigold spoke with unaccustomed deliberation. 'I came across that letter for the first time this morning. At least, I thought it was the first time, it felt like the first time, but it was dated twelve days ago and it was out of its envelope – I couldn't even find the envelope. So I must have read it before. And forgotten all about it. It was all new to me.'

When she was sure she understood, and that there was no more to come for the moment, Adela said, 'You might have opened it and then been interrupted by something and not come across it again till this morning.'

'I'd written "Received 26th October" on it; it must have been a long time in the post, because it was dated the 21st.'

'You still might have been interrupted just after writing it, writing down the date you received the letter.'

'I can't remember writing it or receiving the letter.'

'I shouldn't worry, dear. Things slip my mind all the time. Look at the way I forgot the telephone bill and had us cut off for three days. It was the second time running, too.'

'Adela, that's just forgetfulness. You've always been a bit like that, not a hundred per cent efficient. This is senility.'

'Oh, really, such nonsense. You're the least senile person I know. Of our sort of generation, I mean.'

'I can't stand the thought of ending up a vegetable.'

'Oh, honestly. A lapse of memory over a letter, that's hardly being a vegetable. You must keep a sense of—'

'People don't turn into vegetables overnight, not necessarily anyway. It can be a gradual process and that means it has to start somewhere.'

'Well, dear, at our age we can't expect everything to be just as—'

'We can't expect not to begin falling apart at the seams. How frightfully clever of you to have thought of that. All I can say to you is tunkalunks.' ('Thank you' or 'thanks' in Marigold's very own lexicon.)

'I should have a word with the doctor if you feel . . .'

Adela stopped speaking because Marigold had turned and started walking back towards the house. It was no use going after her: some people might have been able to find the right words of apology and comfort, but Adela knew she was not one of them. She continued for a little way in the original direction. At this time of the year it was hard to find anything worth seeing, apart from deadly nightshade and rowan berries. She looked at them, and heard the song of a blackbird. It lasted only a few seconds; by now, she thought to herself, there could not be much left for him to sing about.

Thirteen

'Gentlemen will please refrain,' sang Shorty to the tune of Dvořák's *Humoresque*, 'from making water while the train, is standing station-airy at the plat-form . . .'

He reeled out of the ground-floor lavatory, dealing himself with the doorpost a buffet that almost sent him back whence he had come, then, after a wide sweep, entered the kitchen. Here, as happened half a dozen times a day, Mr Pastry and Pusscat were locked in their peculiar form of combat, one that started as a mixture of fight and game in about equal proportions, with an escalating trend in favour of the fight element. The dog snarled and began digging his teeth in; the cat, pinned down on her back, yelled and scrabbled at his belly with her hind claws.

'Let her be, you bloody fool,' said the man, and kicked Mr Pastry in the ribs hard enough to cause a sharp howl and an abrupt departure. After he had got up off the rush mat, where the sudden shift of balance involved in the kick had laid him full length, Shorty added to Pusscat, 'And you're a stupid bitch to let things get that far. Need your brains tested.'

He crossed the narrow part of the hall to the foot of the stairs, weaving this way and that like a man in a top-heavy ship. 'Hoboes lying underneath, will get it in the eyes and teeth, and they won't like it any more than you.' The banisters made the ascent less of a directional problem, but put a good deal of strain on the arms. At the top, he stood almost still and considered. He ought to have brought the gardening-tools bottle from the coal-house instead of just swigging out of it. Now it was between the wardrobe bottle and the suitcase bottle. In his present state, unusually advanced for the time of day because of the lunch-time session, he might well bring down the whole wardrobe instead of just what lay on its top. That made it the suitcase. He got himself into the box-room – would have found it difficult to keep himself out once launched towards it – knocked over, not on purpose, one of the many piles of George's books ranged there, tried vainly to restore it, and uncached the Dr Macdonald's. Half full; just right.

In the room he shared with Bernard, he took off his cardigan and trousers, though not his socks, and got into bed. It was a single bed; Bernard's bed, of the same order but higher quality, stood on the far side of an unfolded folding screen; the two men had never shared a bed except to make love, and that not for over thirty-three years. When, in 1946, civilians at last, they had met again for the first time since before the war, Bernard's proposal that they set up together had been very specific on that point. It had been all one to Shorty, who, though finding the physical attentions of men far from unpleasant, had never had much real sexual feeling for them. (He had never had much for women either, come to that; a tart every month or six weeks had seen him through nicely until the whole shooting-match had stopped mattering one way or the other.)

Now he poured something like a gill of booze into the King George V Jubilee mug that had miraculously survived continual use – perhaps not so miraculously, for it was Shorty's boast that, whatever else he might break, a vessel containing liquor was always safe with him, that he had once fallen head-long drink in hand, sprained his left wrist and not spilt a drop.

He sipped, lit a Player's No. 6, sipped again. This was the squaddie's literal seventh heaven: he was dry, warm, indoors, off duty, smoking, pissed, and getting more pissed still. 'And no chance of getting collared for guard,' said Shorty.

Fourteen

Mr Smith and the shoemaker enjoy discussing politics, read Bernard. *The farmer, Mr Butcher and the baker belong to the same bowls club. Mr Farmer is not the smith.* The trouble was, he had got the hang of these things now. But he might as well finish the puzzle as not.

In the past, he had been a man of many interests. The athletic ones – fives, racquets, cricket – had gone when they had had to go and he did not want to read about them. Military tactics and strategy, the history of the Empire, anything concerned with India (the land of his

45

birth and early childhood and of eight years' service between the wars), pioneers in aviation, chess, the life of the Duke of Wellington, the works of George Meredith, all had gone too, thoroughly and for good, even though they had not had to, or not in any obvious sense. To try any of them these days, to look at *Kim* or *The Egoist*, was to come up against something with as little point as a railway-platform conversation between a departing traveller and the man seeing him off. So all he did was pass the time.

He had become quite good at that, having long since proved the importance of rules and limitations. No brain-work of any kind before luncheon: nothing but a long sojourn – from necessity, not choice – on the lavatory, a careful shave, an unhurried bath, minutes spent on the selection of shirt, tie, socks, more minutes on tidying his half of the bedroom, the rest of the period got through with the aid of wireless, tonic-water, cigarettes and doing George. Games only between tea and dinner: bridge problems – nowadays he hated bridge, but did not mind bridge problems – or patience. In this field he had emerged as something of a virtuoso and authority. His exhaustive library on the subject included a first edition (1890) of *Patience Games* by 'Cavendish', once his father's property, and was ready to hand, not incarcerated behind the doors of his bookcase. Finally, after dinner, some sporadic talk, an inattentive glance at television or half-listen-in to the wireless, and dozing.

He solved the puzzle. He would check, although he felt sure he had got it right; he did and had: Mr Shoemaker was the farmer. He could not try another puzzle, not at once. Then it occurred to him that he had not yet read the *Daily Telegraph*, but it was not to be seen. He had put it down somewhere when the Fishwicks arrived. Where? Not in the hall, nor the kitchen. Perhaps Shorty had taken it upstairs to read, or fumble uncomprehendingly through, before he settled down to his Egyptian physical jerks. (His phraseology, like Marigold's, sometimes had the power of acquiring an unwarranted currency in the minds of others.)

In their bedroom, Bernard looked round the edge of the screen at Shorty, who was asleep and had not got the paper anywhere about him. His mouth was open, but he was not snoring. Bernard continued to look at him. Shorty had gone the way of military tactics and the rest through no fault of his. Here was someone whom he, Bernard, granted to deserve a certain respect, not much, perhaps, but some; and, given their shared history, he had a claim on affection as well. It was about five years since Bernard had finally satisfied himself that he had become incapable of either feeling. The incapability held for Adela, George, Marigold – though in her case there had never been the least affection – and anyone else he might run into. There were not many in that last category nowadays. He had purposely missed the last two reunion dinners of his regiment: not the regiment he had been virtually sacked from, the inferior one he had been allowed to join when men were needed in 1939. It was such a business getting to London, and so crowded and noisy when one got there.

He would not have said that he found the company at Tuppenny-hapenny Cottage altogether without savour. There was still a little satisfaction to be had out of scoring off them in talk, but it did seem to be on the decrease. He must see if he could not come up with some less subtle means of venting on the four of them his lack of respect and affection. What had happened, what was the change in his circumstances that had led him to this decision? Well, anyhow, such a project would help to pass the time.

The *Telegraph* was in the kitchen after all, partly concealed by the fruit-bowl which he was nearly sure he had seen Adela removing from the luncheon-table. She would hear about that at dinner.

Fifteen

A few days later, Marigold sat in her room trying to write a letter to her friend Emily Rouse. She found it hard work, she who had always found such activity a durable pleasure, because this morning she was in a state of acute fear. Ever since coming across Emily's letter as if for the first time but in fact for the second, or third, she had not been able to suppress the fear, and a further incident had sharpened it; nevertheless it was worse at the moment because Dr Mainwaring was due to call in response to her summons, and she would have to tell him what had happened and hear what he had to say.

Round her were her numerous possessions, each in its place: fern, footstool, china menagerie, postal scales, cylindrical cushion with tassel, miniature said to be of ancestor and said to be by Cosway, and many a flower-vase, paperweight and candlestick. She ran her eye over them and found them all reassuringly in order; after so many years it failed to take in what would have struck many observers as the most unusual feature of the room, a coverlet divided into six sections, each bearing an incompetently-appliquéd slogan. In order, these ran: *milkie-pilkies*, *sardeenies*, *mousie*, *bunnie-wunnie*, *collar-wallar with bellsie-wellsies*, and *creamie*. They had been in some sense intended to please (even Marigold could not quite have said how) one or other long-forgotten predecessor of Pusscat, who now herself lay in a rough disc on one corner of *bunnie-wunnie*.

There was a faint sound from the front door, then a fist pounded vigorously on it. Marigold looked in the glass to make sure her make-up was properly matt, rehearsed a smile and slipped a charm-bracelet on to her wrist: it was extra important on an occasion like this to be seen absolutely at one's best. As far back as she could remember, she had gone in for day-dreams about what clothes, jewellery and the like she would wear if, like her admired and adored Marie Antoinette, she were somehow to find herself facing public execution. A country GP's visit was hardly on that scale, but the principle held.

Ushered in by Shorty with prolonged and parodied ceremony, the doctor shook hands and sat down on a green-padded chair of uncertain period. Despite his heavy whiskers and inch-wide bracket-shaped moustache, he looked to Marigold about fifteen. Actually he was more than twice that, though he would have confessed, if he had not been so serious-minded and if there had been anybody available to confess it to, that nothing could touch a visit to Tuppenny-hapenny Cottage for making old age seem as remote as interstellar travel.

'What's been the trouble, Mrs Pyke?'

'What has been and is the trouble is that I'm losing my poor little mind, Dr Mainwaring.'

'That seems most unlikely.'

'It's to do with my memory, and letters. I've been forgetting ones I receive and also ones I write. That's much worse, the ones I write. I telephoned your surgery because I found I'd written two letters to the same person, and I was just going to send them off, and I saw them together and so I opened them, and I found they were both answering the same letter from her and they were the same, my letters were, almost word for word.'

The doctor asked for details and got them in full measure. Eventually he said,

'I see. Is this lady a close friend of yours?'

'I've never been clever at all, I haven't got a good brain and it's no use caring now, but I've always been able to sort of keep up with things. It's been my life, keeping up with things, especially the last few years, and if I can't do that I can't do anything; there'd be nothing for me to do, and I couldn't bear that. I'd have to go away somewhere; I couldn't let them, you know, all of them see it. I couldn't bear it.'

'I appreciate that.' Dr Mainwaring recognized his patient's departure from her habitual style, but was just as good at hiding the pity the departure made him feel as he was at hiding the irritation the habitual style made him feel. 'It's important that you answer my question, Mrs Pyke. The lady you were writing to – are you very close friends? Old friends?'

'Not specially. We've known each other a long time, but never very well.'

'Now: remember we're talking in confidence. Would you call her one of the most interesting people you know?'

'No, I don't think I would. But she's most frightfully sweetle-peetles.'

Acquainted as he was with Marigold's lingo, the doctor only just managed not to scream or to pitch forward on to the tasteful orange-and-buff carpet (once an ornament of her home in Beauchamp Place). If challenged, he would have said that, among the very few generalizations medical practice had suggested to him, there was a fairly obvious one about people in genuine fear (as now) casting aside all affectation: mention X-rays and barium meals, his partner had put it to him the previous week with his immediate agreement, and they stop watching themselves. Here, he thought he saw, was an exception, and hurriedly comforted himself with what he knew to be popularizing notions of how it was the exceptional that was the truly instructive. At the same moment he caught a passing sight of the cat-oriented coverlet, viewed before but never fully assimilated, and himself experienced a twinge of genuine fear compounded with incredulity. Feeling rather as if he had somebody's hand clapped over his mouth, he said,

'So you . . . may have known her a longish . . . time without ever in fact knowing her very well. I think my general reaction would . . . be this.'

This proved to be a long monologue on how everybody tended to forget things that did not really concern them, how the tendency tended to increase with age, how another tendency saw to it that, well, older people found it harder to concentrate, how the two tendencies between them could cause lapses of memory, how in such cases (he went carefully here) there was no reason to expect any significant deterioration, and how he would prescribe some pills which would reduce anxiety and so enable the situation to appear in better perspective. It sounded good and contained no flat lies.

Before the doctor had finished, Shorty came in with coffee and biscuits on a bent silver tray. He stayed a little longer than was altogether necessary, constantly glancing at Marigold in a way the doctor saw as indicating concern and Marigold herself as pretended concern hiding utter indifference, but in fact amounted to pretended concern hiding hostile curiosity: if there was anything wrong with her more than being a snobbish old bitch eaten up with her own importance, he wanted to be one of the first to know about it. He soon saw, however, that Marigold was not going to proclaim that leprosy had just been diagnosed in her or that she was near death from an ingrowing toenail, and neither was the doctor; Adela, later, might have something to tell.

'While I'm here I might as well have a word with you, Mr Shortell,' said Dr Mainwaring.

'Nothing the matter with me, doc, bar anno domini, and from all I hear there's not much to be done about that.'

'Just the same, I think I'd better see you for a minute before I go.'

'You're the boss. I'll be in the kitchen.'

Shorty took himself off. The doctor finished his monologue by saying,

'Well, Mrs Pyke, I want you to remember what I've said and think it over, and take the pills regularly – that's important. I hope I've managed to reassure you a little.'

'Oh, absolutely; you've been quite marvellous. I feel so differently about the whole thing. It's frightfully kind of you to take all this trouble over a silly old woman.'

Dr Mainwaring saw that he had indeed reassured his patient a little.

Sixteen

Adela was next. She told the doctor she was feeling about the same as usual and at once went on to inquire about Marigold.

'No great cause for concern there, Miss Bastable. You could help by discussing the situation with her and generally helping her to calm down. But as regards your own—'

'It means so much to her, do you see, this business of staying in touch with everyone. Her correspondence – it's like a City firm. She gets letters by every post. You must do something to help her, Dr Mainwaring.'

'Well, I hope I've—'

'But I'm sure she's got a lot of confidence in you. We all have, of course. Do please look in on Professor Zeyer, won't you? I think you'll see a great change in him. For the better, I mean.'

They stood in Adela's north-facing bedroom, round which the doctor looked while she went into considerable detail about George. Apart from some tea-mugs of royal or regional connection, unused ashtrays, eroded postcards and other presumable mementos, he half noticed, as he had on previous visits, a great many photographs, in frames or pinned to a cork backing. Apart from one of the lesser-known London hospitals and a house in some non-European locale, the subjects were chiefly women, chiefly in the dress of one or another bygone era. On a cursory inspection, portrayals of the occupant of the room were nowhere to be seen, very likely as a result of self-effacement.

'That sounds most encouraging,' said the doctor when he had the chance to. 'But I don't want you to over-exert yourself. You must remember your own—'

'Oh, there's no real exertion involved. My brother gives Mr Short-ell and me a hand to get Professor Zeyer upstairs again. It's funny how his bad leg seems to sort of come and go. My brother's leg.'

It would have taken a better-informed and even more attentive listener than the doctor to hear that Adela was unsardonically aware of the regular shifts in the condition of her brother's leg: bad whenever bringing George downstairs was on the cards, wondrously improved when it came to getting him back upstairs.

'I'll talk to your brother too, of course. But you must tell me about yourself, Miss Bastable. Any increase in pain? Any unusual discomfort?'

'Oh, not really, no. I'm as strong as a horse.'

Seventeen

George was next. He was full of enthusiasm about his return to work. The doctor listened approvingly, but felt he had to say,

'You should remember that, even with all this assistance, you're still exerting yourself considerably when you move about.'

'You mean I'm in danger of another stroke.'

'I wouldn't be doing my job if I said any different, Professor Zeyer. There are two points, really. One is that any sort of strain must be avoided within reason. The other is, if you follow that advice you're in no more danger than anybody else with your medical history.'

'Take it easy, in fact.'

'That's right.'

'I'll remember,' said George, not at all daunted by what he had heard. Work counted more than mobility, more than anything; Adela had not yet had time to get him his new typewriter, but he had already drafted his Mihailović letter in his mind, and a few days' delay would make no difference to a quarterly journal.

Bernard was next. To him, the doctor said,

'As before, Mr Bastable?'

'Yes.'

'Mr Brownjohn's a good man.'

'Unbelievable name, that. I do very much wonder how he came by it – I should say, how his ancestor came by it. Gossip in the village, do you think?'

'I expect so. We'll be in touch.'

Shorty was last. In deference to the doctor, he had so far that day drunk only one small tumbler of that other doctor's potation, although it was nearly noon. He said,

'Well, any hope of a death in the family?'

'Everybody's doing as well as can be expected.'

'Oh, terrific.'

'Let's take a look at that liver of yours.'

'What for? It hasn't been playing me up.'

'By the time you notice there's something wrong there'll already have been permanent damage. You don't want to end up like Mr Bastable.'

'True, O king.'

Upstairs, Shorty took his trousers and underpants down and lay on his bed while the doctor kneaded the relevant part of his abdomen.

'How much do you drink a day?'

'About a bottle.' There were in existence, after all, bottles that would hold the true amount.

'Not a bottle of spirits?'

'No fear. Kind of wine.'

'Well, there is some enlargement, but it doesn't seem to have increased since last time, and if you stick to one bottle of wine a day and eat plenty of meat and fish and chicken, you should be all right.'

'Message received and understood.'

The doctor went back to Marigold for a final word, and Shorty was not far behind, ostensibly to collect the coffee-tray, so he had a good

view when, in the course of seeing the doctor to the door, she fell flat
on her back as abruptly as if she had been shot. The two men, each
with every appearance of solicitude, helped her to her feet. She
seemed shaken but unhurt.

'I trod on something . . .'

'There.' Shorty picked up a tennis ball, much discoloured and not
easy to see in the hall with its single undersized window, even at
midday. The ball was also damp and considerably lacerated.

Bernard appeared from the sitting-room, no doubt drawn to the
scene by the sound of Marigold's fall. 'Nothing wrong, I hope?'

'Nasty toss she took,' said Shorty. 'Towser's flaming ball.'

'That damned dog.'

'Are you sure you're all right, Mrs Pyke?' asked Dr Mainwaring.

'It's old and disgusting and it ought to be put down. It's always
bullying my poor little cat.'

'He means a lot to George,' said Shorty.

A reflective look crossed Bernard's heavy face.

Eighteen

One evening later that week, Shorty, Marigold and Adela were gathered in the sitting-room. Shorty was doing his best to read a
paperback book that told, it seemed to him, of some men on a
wartime mission to blow something up. His state of mind, normal
for him at this time of day, lent the narrative an air of deep mystery.
New characters kept on making unceremonious appearances, or,
more exactly, he would find that he had been in a sense following
their activities for several pages without having noticed their arrival,
or, more exactly still, they would turn out, on consultation of the
first couple of chapters, to have been about the place from the start.
The prose style was tortuous, elliptic, allusive, full of strange poet-
icisms; the dialogue, after the same fashion, was stuffed with
obscurities and non-sequiturs and, like the story itself, constantly
referred to people, events, places and the rest that had never come

up before, or, once again, had come up eight or eighty pages earlier. Every so often he would run across some detail that nearly convinced him he had read the whole thing before, perhaps more than once. But none of that bothered him in the least: he was not working for an exam, and to read as he did meant that he used up books very slowly and economically.

Marigold too, in her different way, was contentedly reading. Dr Mainwaring's pills must already have started to take effect; at any rate, she had been pretty tranquil for the past forty-eight hours or so; there had been no recurrence, as far as she was aware, of loss of memory. What she was reading was her scrap-book, a compilation mainly of short items referring to persons far from squarely in the public eye, persons not always known to her in any direct fashion, persons who had less often done something than had something happen to them.

Only Adela, of the three, was less than at ease. A few minutes earlier, she had given up trying to watch the little Japanese television set: there was a young man singing and moving about a lot on one channel, cowboys on another, and what had turned out to be an incomprehensible drama of some sort on the third. It was incomprehensible to her partly because she could not with confidence differentiate any one character from any other, except in point of sex, and partly because, as had been clearly announced at the start of the transmission but too quickly or unemphatically to register with her, what she had seen was part of the fourth episode of a six-part serial.

She picked up her book, *Sense and Sensibility*, but did not open it. Bernard had gone to London that morning for an exhaustive medical examination by somebody called Mr Brownjohn, promising to telephone from Newmarket railway station when he had returned there and needed her to bring him home in her car. Probably about six o'clock, he had said; it was now nearly eight, and eight was dinner-time, as he well knew. Something must be wrong. She could not read: it was not enough of a distraction.

'What can have happened?' asked Adela.

'Aw, hell, babe,' said Shorty. 'Guy gets held up some on the railroad, okay? So it don't mean no bunch of bad hombres ain't wrecked the train. Maybe he just don't done gotten the time to call you-all from that old sheriff's office, see what I mean, mm-hm?'

'They must have sort of kept him in, decided they'd got to operate on him straight away or something.'

'Look, Aleda, Adela, bad news travels fast. If there was any question of that, we'd have heard hours back.'

'It'll be those swine of railwaymen having a go-slow or a work-to-rule or whatever it is,' said Marigold placidly. 'Pack of rotten Reds.'

'But he said he'd telephone.'

'Like I said, Adela, even the Queen can't telephone from a perishing railway carriage.'

'She probably can, don't you think? I was reading somewhere that people do from cars these days. All right, I see what you mean . . . Listen.'

A motor vehicle could be heard approaching. Adela ran into the hall, Shorty following more slowly. Marigold turned a page of her scrap-book.

'. . . got a taxi,' said Bernard a moment later as he came into the room. He was wearing a dark suit and tie and looked like an eminent greengrocer.

'But it can't be out of order,' said Adela warmly. 'I thought of that and got the operator to ring me and it worked.'

'Well, anyhow, I couldn't get through. Not that it matters.'

'How did it go, Bernard?' asked Shorty.

'Oh yes, how did it go?'

Bernard smiled, and not caustically at that. 'Clean bill. For my age, that is, of course. Furthermore—'

'Oh, Bernard, dear . . .'

Adela could not resist embracing her brother, who for once (she could not remember the last time) did not stiffen and hold himself away.

'Good show, Bernard,' said Shorty.

'You must be frightfully relieved,' said Marigold.

Shorty suppressed a grin. People who sound insincere all the time, he thought to himself, should not expect others to notice the difference when they try to sound insincere.

'Furthermore,' Bernard was going on, 'the excellent Mr Brownjohn said he saw no reason why I shouldn't start drinking again, in reasonable quantities. He seemed to think it would be positively beneficial. Something to do with the circulation.'

'He of the brown john hath spoken great words of wisdom and good cheer,' said Shorty. 'What do you fancy, Bernard?'

'I've been thinking about little else ever since the Brownjohn declaration. Is there any gin in the house?'

'There is, externally cobwebbed, true, but doubtless unimpaired.'

'I'd like some with about the—'

'About the same amount of water and nothing else. I remember.'

While Shorty was out of the room, Adela said, 'So you found the place all right,' and, as soon as she realized what she had said, braced herself for the 'It would indeed appear so' or alternatively the 'No, I spent the day walking the streets in a fruitless search' that would have been Bernard's normal response. But he said only,

'Yes, went straight to it without any trouble at all.'

She smiled. 'You're a different man already, Bernard.'

'Yes, I think perhaps I am.'

'You must have been worrying a lot.'

'I suppose I was.'

'We all understand. Tell me,' – and she asked some questions about his day which he answered.

Shorty came back with Bernard's drink in his hand and a similar amount inside him. 'One London Dry Gin and water, *Sir*!'

'Thank you, my man. Well . . . here's to me.' He sipped, then frowned. 'What brand is this?'

Shorty told him.

'They've done something to it: it doesn't taste as it used to.'

'You've forgotten it, Bernard,' said Shorty; 'your mouth's out of practice.'

'Perhaps it is.'

'You keep on with it and you'll be all right.'

Nineteen

Christmas approached. Bernard and Shorty on one occasion, and Marigold on another, were ferried to Newmarket to buy their presents. George bought his by proxy: Adela's through Shorty, everyone else's through Adela.

It was a busy time for Marigold. Her having done her Christmas shopping at the little local stores was in the interests of economy of both cash and physical effort: she had very little of the one, and what she knew to be not an inexhaustible fund of the other. She did make two trips to London, to visit old and largely or wholly immobile connections of hers; but most of her days were passed in dispatching Christmas cards – more accurately, Christmas letters, because every card bore a personal message, often of some length. An eighty-six-year-old lady in Clapham, who had once taught Marigold history, was puzzled to receive two almost identical communications of this sort on successive days; her mental condition, however, saw to it that her puzzlement was neither deep nor lasting. Over this period, Marigold told Adela several things two or three times over, but on each occasion Adela managed not to tell her she had done so.

George was busy too, though not on any Yuletide matters. Through Adela, again, he exchanged typewriters, and on his new machine slowly but effectively typed his Mihailović letter, which was not acknowledged. He also, as planned, wrote to several periodicals in search of work as a reviewer. Some answered that there was nothing for him just then; others intimated that no man could tell how far in the future lay the moment when there might be something for him. He was put out, but not put off. There was surely room for a popular history of central Europe between the beginnings of the Munich crisis and, say, the Prague coup of 1948. Among his files or in his memory, he had a good deal of unpublished material which would have been out of place in a work of scholarship, but would lend colour and immediacy to the kind of book he was contemplating. Not that he merely contemplated it for long: he was soon engaged on a synopsis and the drafting of a specimen chapter. To his deep gratitude, Shorty acted as his librarian, taking lists of books to the box-room and quite often coming back with the right ones.

On his own account, Shorty was not especially busy during this period, dividing his day as usual between housework, gardening and getting drunk.

Bernard, who on his shopping expedition had bought several items not selected as Christmas presents, turned quite busy thereafter.

The approach of the festive season meant that Adela was busier than ever.

Twenty

'*Such* a pity it hasn't lasted,' said Marigold one afternoon about the middle of December. 'After we all thought he'd got so much better.'

Adela looked at her in sudden fear. 'What's happened? He told us he was all right. That man in London—'

'I don't mean physically, angel. I'd have thought it was obvious I didn't mean *physically*. I mean the way he goes on, the way he treats everyone, including you. He's just as offensive and intolerable as he ever was. It lasted precisely ten days, the improvement, when he behaved like a human being for a change. Then, absolutely overnight, he—'

'I think it was the drink, dear. That is, he was so looking forward to a glass of gin or wine or something, just an occasional one, and then he found he didn't enjoy it and it made him feel dizzy and everything. So I suppose he . . . feels he's back where he was before he saw the man.'

The two women's discussion of Bernard was taking place in the woods near the cottage. As they walked, the sun, unusually strong for the time of year, lit up the bare branches and stalks, and, whenever they came to a spot sheltered from the faint breeze, communicated slight but perceptible heat.

'I think it was George that did it,' said Marigold abruptly. 'And that dog of his. He was bearable before they turned up.'

'But poor George can't help—'

'You cast your mindle-pindle back and think about it and you'll see I'm right. Anyway, that's neither here nor there. The point is, I doubt if I can stand it much longer. All this hostility and peevishness and . . . I think I'll have to find somewhere else to go. Make other arrangements.'

In fact, Marigold did not especially object to the restoration (real enough) of Bernard's habitual behaviour, and had been continuing to enjoy in a small way her opportunities of getting back at him and getting at Shorty. Her gathering resolve to quit the household matched the progress of her amnesia, fits of which now came upon her at least daily. To hide her condition from the others, especially Bernard, as best she might, and as long as she could, she kept to her room more than formerly. Dr Mainwaring's prescription had not cured her aversion from the prospect of becoming hopelessly senile in the company of people who knew her, nor had it weakened her conviction that senility was her fate. The pills had done no more than allow her to remain calm when she noted her lapses of memory and when she considered what to do.

Blinking rapidly, Adela said, 'But you can't do that, Marigold. Where would you go?'

'I've one or two ideas.' The previous year, Marigold had visited a friend in a sort of old people's home in North London. For what it was, it was not too bad a place, and the friend would be no embarrassment, having shortly afterwards had to leave for a hospital where those who could do nothing for themselves were taken care of. As for money, the sale of almost everything she possessed would start her off, and she could rely on Trevor and Keith to follow up, rather than have to look after her themselves.

'But . . . breaking everything up just because Bernard's sarcastic sometimes . . .' Adela felt not only despair, but some incredulity; she did not see the import of her brother's behaviour as clearly as Marigold did. 'Oh, I don't mean he isn't sarcastic, but you mustn't take it so seriously. I'll talk to Bernard – he's not completely unreasonable – he'll see . . .'

Marigold, having remembered just in time what reason she had given for her desire to leave, said, 'Oh, it's not only Bernard. That disgusting little squirt Shortell . . .'

'Who makes your bleeding bed and dusts your bleeding furniture and cooks half your bleeding meals and washes up your bleeding dishes,' said Shorty under his breath. He had not intended to eavesdrop, but his approach, over thickly-strewn dead leaves, had been silent, and he had found himself in hearing and out of sight at the same time.

'Oh, I know he's uncouth and drunken and all that . . .'

('Ta muchly, I'm sure.')

'. . . but I couldn't run the house without him.' Adela went into some detail here, ending with a promise to talk to Shorty also. Marigold gave no sign of having listened to any of this. It came to Adela quite clearly that there was nothing more she could say in order to persuade the other not to do as she had threatened. Most women, most people in this situation, would have said, or at least considered saying, 'Won't you stay for my sake?' But it did not occur to her. All she did say was, hesitantly,

'It's definite, then, is it, dear?'

'Oh, I haven't decided yet.' If she became no worse, or only a little worse, and as long as Bernard remained ignorant of what had happened to her, Marigold would not go. With all its shortcomings, Tuppenny-hapenny Cottage was more comfortable and, it could even be said, more cheerful than the North London place. She had raised the question that afternoon so that, in case things went the other way, her pretended motive for departure might seem more convincing. No one must know her real one.

'I see,' said Adela. How many times since she had known her must Marigold have said she had not decided yet? – whether or not she would come to tea, come for a bathe, come to the theatre, come to live here in the first place, come for a walk. Some people by nature found it harder than others to decide things.

'That's right, keep her hanging,' said Shorty, when the two had started to move slowly back towards the house. 'Eh'm afraid Eh haven't desayded yet and yooh can sweat it out in the meantame. Up your arsle-parcel. You wait. It'll be fun. Goldie.'

Twenty-One

'So could you possibly try? It's not a lot to ask, after all, just not snubbing her so much. You needn't put yourself out. It's not as if you're still worrying about your health. You've no real excuse.'

Adela honestly believed that these points, put as she had put them, were best calculated to win Bernard over, and that she had spoken in the gentle, conciliatory tone which something in her, perhaps her very speech-organs, forbade her from ever attaining. It was in direct response to the slightly domineering effect she actually produced that, years ago, Bernard had begun to form his own ironical style. But he said now,

'True. I know I'm a brute sometimes. It's like a habit one falls into, so I suppose one can get out of it too. I promise you I will try.'

He spoke with sincerity. He had several reasons for wanting Marigold to remain in the house, even though concern for his sister's welfare was not one of them. For all that, the genuineness of his feeling somehow communicated itself to her. She smiled and said as animatedly as she could,

'Thank you, dear. I'm so sorry your drinks don't agree with you.'

'So am I. But the way to look at it is that at least that means I don't have more than about one a day, which would please the valuable Brownjohn.'

'It's marvellous of you to take it like that. Well, I must be going. I've got to collect the pensions. There are such queues in the post office these days. Christmas seems to start earlier and earlier every year. As regards people posting their parcels and cards and buying stamps, I mean.'

'Yes, I know what you mean.'

Adela went. Bernard collected the radio from the sitting-room and took it up to his bedroom, in accordance with a recently-established routine: he had explained a couple of times that resting his leg on his bed for an extra hour or so seemed to help it a bit, and it was known that he often listened to the radio in the mornings, or kept it turned on. He turned it on now and found some music or other, but made no move to rest his leg. Far from that, he took up a position by the door that gave him a narrow view of the landing, and waited, farting occasionally in an incisive, military way.

Some minutes passed. Then a door shut downstairs and steps crossed the hall. Hurriedly, Bernard turned up the volume on the transistor, returned to his post, and soon saw Marigold's figure cross his field of vision. Another, nearer, door shut. He made a note of the time in his diary, finding that it lay within a few minutes of the same occasion on previous mornings. Marigold's bowels evidently followed a pretty strict routine, which was more than could be said for some others'. Good.

When, some more minutes later, a period he again noted, she had returned downstairs, he let the radio continue to produce its noises and went along to George's room. He knocked and entered rather abruptly, with the hoped-for result that Mr Pastry raised his faltering growl.

'Oh dear oh dear,' said Bernard in a resonant mutter; then, changing rather than raising his voice, went on, 'Morning, George: how's things?'

'Things are all right.' Clumsily, George pulled his typewriter off his lap.

'I'm not interrupting your work, I hope?'

'No no, rather not, I've got all the time in the world. No deadlines these days, thank God.'

'Yes, I can see it must be a relief. But I think it's splendid you've been able to take up writing again like this, under these conditions.'

'Oh, conditions could be far worse than these, I assure you. Shorty fetches me anything I need to read, and this thing here is very manageable apart from putting in new pieces, and of course much easier for me than using the old way. Most of the writing stuff used to go over my hands or what I was wearing or the things on the bed rather than on what I was supposed to be doing.'

Bernard had worked his way round to the further side of the bed, followed by Mr Pastry, on whose feet he made several attempts to step, this in the hope of provoking further growls or other untoward behaviour: no success. With his face turned towards the window, he said,

'I'm afraid your old hound isn't what you might call at the peak of his popularity these days.'

'I'm sorry to hear that. What's he been up to?'

'Well, he always seems to want to be let in the moment he's let out and the other way round. And then he gives that cat of Marigold's a hell of a time, not that that matters much to me, quite frankly. But recently it looks as if he's taken to crapping inside the house, which is rather a pest. I cleared up a pile of turds yesterday afternoon.'

'Oh, Lord. Are you sure they weren't Pusscat's?'

'No, but I don't think so. I'd prefer not to go into details.'

'Oh, I am so sorry. What a bore for you.'

'He's getting on, isn't he?'

'Well, he's fifteen.'

'Seven fifteens are a hundred and five. That's older than most of us get.'

'That's just a saying, one dog year's equal to seven man years.'

Bernard did not answer at once. He looked, or appeared to look, more directly out of the window. Then he said in his dragging voice,

'According to Marigold, he ought to be put down.'

'You know Marigold. She exaggerates and speaks without thinking all the time.'

'I'm only telling you what she told me. Mind you, George, I doubt if Shorty's exactly mad about him. He does give him a certain amount of extra work, after all.'

The left half of George's mouth grew tense. 'How do you feel yourself?'

'Oh . . . I don't really . . . I probably shouldn't have mentioned it.'

'Why did you?'

'I suppose I wanted to give you the chance of preparing a defence, so to speak,' said Bernard, scolding himself for not having thought of this obvious point in advance. 'In case the animal loses esteem any further.'

'I see. Thank you.'

When Bernard had gone, George beat the flat of his left hand on the bed, and Mr Pastry, after an initial delay and at the second attempt, responded by jumping up to lie beside his master. In George's affections, dogs, animals of any sort, occupied an immovably lower place than any human being he was attached to; nevertheless, they had that place. Mr Pastry was not the most agreeable dog he had owned, but he was agreeable, and, with the intermittent exception of Shorty, there were no human beings at hand to feel affection towards: George had tried and failed to feel anything warmer than gratitude and esteem for Adela. With his widowhood, a large part of his life had been cut out and thrown away somewhere beyond all knowledge. The departure of Mr Pastry would not be remotely a comparable loss, but, again, he was irreplaceable – doubly so, for a virtually bedridden man could never cope with a puppy, nor expect others to cope on his behalf, and a grown dog would not be his dog.

Who could be trusted to fight for Mr Pastry's retention? Adela and, in his sober fits, Shorty. Not enough, perhaps, to stand up against Marigold and Bernard. Time and chance would tell; nothing else.

Twenty-Two

In the coal-house of the cottage there were, besides a small, unchanging pile of coal and various bits of debris, a water-tap, a ladder and a bucket, items used by Shorty when he cleaned the outsides of the windows. Bernard drew water into the bucket, glanced round carefully to make sure he was unobserved, and carried it to the clearing in the woods, where he set it down. Then, his hand moving fast and cleanly for a man of his age, he drew from inside his jacket an object resembling a pistol and aimed it at a nearby clump of laurel. After a short pause, he returned it to a shoulder-holster. This consisted chiefly of a leather-like plastic material, though, having been designed for a juvenile shoulder, it had had to have its strap effectively lengthened with a piece of string. Bernard repeated his quick-drawing exercise some dozens of times before going on to practice no. 2.

He filled the pistol with water from the bucket (for it was a water-pistol) and discharged it at the tree-stump from fifteen paces. At the start he overshot – the thing had a flatter trajectory than he had expected – but corrected his aim well before the jet was spent. After half an hour of further attempts at varying distances, he considered he had a fair mastery of the weapon. In his Service days he had been an excellent revolver-shot, had indeed saved his own life in 1917 thereby, and was not put off by the slight breeze that sometimes took him wide of his mark: direction was not important – he knew he could handle that, even with a moving target. What counted was elevation, and here he was greatly helped by the fact that, as when firing tracer from a machine-gun, misses could be rectified in mid-burst. It was consoling to find that hand and eye were still relatively unimpaired, even if the enterprise for which they were now needed might strike some as odd or trivial.

Practice no. 3 combined the first two: quick-draw-and-fire in one movement, often accompanied by a half-turn of the body to one flank or the other. Some minutes of this, and of bending and straightening each time the pistol needed a recharge, quickened his breathing and heartbeat and brought him out in a light sweat – but pleasurably, so that he remembered for a moment what it had felt like to begin to warm up in a game of racquets. At last he restored the pistol (filled) to its holster, emptied the remains of the water and started back to the house. He was almost there when the sudden appearance of Adela, returned from the village, sent him diving for cover at a speed he had not tried for years. The pistol was under his coat; the empty bucket could easily be explained, or left unexplained; it was instinct, the spirit of the thing. That morning, he felt, he had done a little more than pass the time.

Twenty-Three

It was just after one p.m. towards the end of the week before Christmas. In the kitchen were Adela, Shorty and George. Adela was opening some plastic packets of a kind of ham that also bore a plastic appearance; she knew it was not very nice, but it was protein, it filled people up, and its price had just been slashed by 1½p per packet.

Shorty was stooped by the hearth, working on the fire with a leaky pair of bellows. George sat at the table; it was the second of what had become established as his two weekly days downstairs. Theoretically, he could have made such appearances every day there was, but he did not want to wear out his welcome, already (he rather fancied) losing its first freshness with Bernard, and there was his work. Without much wanting to, simply, as always, anxious not to appear sullen or bored, he said,

'I was reading where a chap wrote this morning, I expect you saw it yesterday, about those four young swine who broke into the place to rob it, but there was hardly any money in where they keep the money, because the boss had just been and paid it in, so they hit him with a tightening-up affair and the iron business for the fire and so on, and took the money in what he was wearing and how you tell the time and even his smoking stuff. What can you do about people like that?'

'I suppose you rush them to hospital,' said Adela, making mustard. 'These days they can—'

'Hospital? There's nothing wrong with them in that sense. They're just—'

'I think George means the thugs, Adela.'

'Oh, I see, of course.'

'But isn't it appalling behaviour?'

'Dreadful.'

'Really frightening, George,' said Shorty, thinking that the other had a very fair point, one that might well make an audience of homicidal maniacs properly sit up and take notice. A pity Bernard was not on the spot to appreciate it. 'Shall I fetch the others, Adela?' He put the bellows down on the iron fender.

'Well, that's up to you,' said Adela, looking at them. 'They leak too, don't they, the others? I must get—'

'I really meant fetch Bernard and Marigold for lunch, actually.'

'Oh.' This time, Adela sounded as Bernard sometimes did in this kind of one-down situation, loftily disappointed at such a trite answer to what on the face of it was a not uninteresting problem. 'Yes, I suppose so. If you would.'

Shorty had just adopted the minor crouch necessary to get through the doorway when an approaching series of barks was heard, followed by an approaching patter of animal feet, closely followed by Pusscat very closely followed by Mr Pastry, soon afterwards followed by Marigold, eventually and finally followed by Bernard. He was in time to see Marigold clutching her pet to her in what even a stranger to our civilization would have recognized as a protective attitude while the dog, with many a snuffle, trotted round the room at an evident loss and George remonstrated with him. There was some tension.

'That damned dog.'

'It's only a game, Bernard,' said Shorty. 'He wouldn't hurt her, not him. Not really hurt her.'

'Oh, wouldn't he?' Marigold glared hard.

'How did he get out?' asked George. 'I thought he was shut up in the sitting-room.'

Shorty glanced at Bernard, but said nothing.

'Somebody must have left the door open,' said Adela.

'The creature's becoming intolerable.' Bernard turned to Marigold. 'Surely you must agree.'

Privately she did, and in full measure, but to express agreement with Bernard was so foreign to her instinct and practice that she confined herself to further crooning over her cat.

'Just like him chasing his ball,' said Shorty. 'I allude, of course, to the tennis version thereof. Come on, Bonzo, my lad, you'd better get out while the going's good.'

He took Mr Pastry by the collar and hauled him from the kitchen. Bernard, with a dissatisfied air, took his place at the head of the table. George could see the case for letting the incident blow over, but, in the silence, found himself saying,

'I really must apologize for the wretched old fellow.' He tried to keep his tone light. 'And I do appreciate the way you all put up with him. If I could do anything myself, I would, but I'm—'

'Granted as soon as asked,' said Shorty, now doling out plates of ham. He continued in song, 'How much is that dog-gy in the window? The one with the waggully tay-yool. How much—'

'Potatoes here, Shorty,' said Adela.

During the meal, there was some talk about Christmas, held together chiefly by the fact that what was said concerned Christmas in one way or another.

'Of course, at my grandfather's it was Christmas *breakfast* that was the real occasion,' said Marigold.

'Of course,' said Bernard. 'What else? Sorry, do go on.'

'Thank you. There was game and venison and herrings and troutle-poutles and kidneys and bacon and great farm eggs and fresh-baked bread and gallons and gallons of home-brewed beer. Literally hundreds of people used to come from all over the county. I remember one year – I can't have been more than ten or eleven – the bishop came, and he didn't care for the rector, do you see, and he was a great big fellow, the bishop, and do you know what he did?'

'Yes, as a matter of fact I do, Marigold,' said Shorty, pulling a piece of gristle from between his teeth. 'He got so pissed he saddled up the poor bloody rector and rode him round the dining-room belting him with his riding-crop. You told us the whole story last night.'

All except George looked at Bernard, but he was sawing theatrically at a slice of ham, had shut off his attention as soon as he saw a fresh dose of Marigold's cackle on the way, had delivered his token barb and relapsed into day-dreaming about the projects he had in train.

Into another silence, George said, 'In Pilsen we used to go in for . . .' He stopped when he found himself faced by devising on-the-spot periphrases for a whole mental shelf-load of commodities whose names, at the best of times, would have come to him more readily in Czech than in English; but he went on quite quickly, and he thought rather adroitly, '. . . all manner of stuff I'm sure you couldn't get hold of now unless you were a Party boss.'

'I remember Vera saying how she used to look forward to it for weeks every year, to Christmas, I mean,' said Adela, who had noticed that her brother was a little more displeased with events than usual, and who still, in the teeth of a third of a century's worth of evidence pointing hard the other way, believed that an affectionate reference to his late wife must have a softening effect on him.

This did reach Bernard. 'You must be mixing her up with someone else.' He sounded puzzled, driven to this conclusion against his will.

'When she discussed the matter with me, on what I remember as a single occasion and for about thirty seconds in all, she said the whole thing bored her stiff. In fact, I think I can do better than that. Yes – an interest in Christmas is natural in children and something like to be pitied when old people have it, but in anybody else it's a mark of gullibility and credulity and one thing and another. Something very much along those lines. What the devil is the matter with you, George?'

'Sorry,' said George, who had been laughing almost silently and shaking his head for ten seconds or so, 'but you're the one who's doing the mixing up. No Czech would say that, not one of Vera's generation anyway. Who do you think invented Good King Wenceslas? No, the person who used to go round saying that was one of her so-called emancipated friends from over here. I've an idea . . . If you'll give me a minute I'll come up with her name.'

Bernard breathed hard. 'I can recall the scene exactly. That rather vulgar house in West Harnham. I was at my davenport doing the Christmas cards, and Vera came in from—'

'Bobs Butterfield! Bobs Butterfield! Rather small, Titian-haired type of girl, used to paint her nails and put too much rouge on her cheeks. Bobs Butterfield. I haven't even thought of her for thirty years. Well, the old brain can't be in too bad a state if it can reach back as far as that.'

'I haven't the slightest recollection of any such person.'

'Well, I'm sure you could catch me out on a lot of things too. Do you remember her, Shorty? Just as a matter of interest.'

'I didn't have much to do with what you might call the social side in those days, George.'

'No, I suppose not,' said George tolerantly. 'Bobs Butterfield. That's right. She was a great one for getting away from Victorian attitudes. I wonder if she's still going on about them.'

'Very possibly,' said Bernard. 'Vera said to me what I told you she said to me.'

'I'm sorry.' George was shaking his head again. 'She wouldn't have.'

'To you she may well never have done. To me she did, on the occasion I described just now.'

'Ah, I think I've got it. I *think* I can explain the whole thing in a way acceptable to all. Vera was telling you *what Bobs Butterfield had said to her* about Christmas, and you missed that part because you were busy with the cards and thought Vera was saying *what she herself* thought.'

'No. No.'

'Well, I distinctly remember her telling me she loved Christmas,' said Adela. 'Vera telling me, I mean.'

'We like Christmas, don't we, Pusscat?' whispered Marigold.

'I'm dreaming of a white Christmas,' sang Shorty, 'just like the—'

'She hated Christmas,' said Bernard. He tried to stop his head trembling.

'I'm sorry,' said George again. 'She didn't.'

'You're not questioning my good faith, you just mean I'm honestly mistaken. Is that it?'

'Exactly. After all, I did know her much longer than you did.'

For a moment, Bernard felt real regret at what must now actually happen to Mr Pastry. It was only for a moment, because Marigold, in a breathy murmur that George, for one, found hard to follow, said into the air,

'I think it's nicer to remember people for what they liked rather than for what they didn't like.'

'What?' said Bernard on a long, steady note.

'I said it's nicer to remember people for what they liked than for what they didn't like,' said Marigold in the closest approach to a yell she was capable of, which was close.

Bernard's reply would have reached the rearmost file of a battalion in column, had one been arrayed before him; even Shorty was impressed. 'Perhaps it is and perhaps it isn't, but one can't remember what didn't take place, and I know it's late in life for you to start speaking at a normal level, but for God's sake try.'

He left the room, limping heavily.

'I'm sorry, dear,' said Adela to Marigold; 'he's sensitive about being a bit deaf.'

'And I'm sensitive about being shouted at.'

'I'll have a word with him.'

'You've had words with him before and a fat lot of good they've done. I can't stand it any longer, living in the same house as that man. I shall have to start making definite plans.'

Marigold went out too. In fact she was not offended; on the contrary, making Bernard lose his temper had toned her up, and she still felt relief almost to the point of elation at his having missed her lapse about her grandfather and the bishop. But the lapse itself was an unfavourable sign; her parting words in the kitchen had been intended as additional cover, should she finally be compelled to leave.

'I shouldn't worry too much, Adela,' said Shorty. 'I reckon she's a sight too comfortable where she is to really think of shifting.'

'Oh, I do hope you're right.'

'Mind you, she's an odd piece, the madam is.'

'I suppose I may have been a bit tactless, going on about Vera like that,' said George.

'Yes, George, you may have.'

Twenty-Four

On the morning of Christmas Eve, Bernard was in the sitting-room as usual. He remained altogether idle until, just after eleven o'clock, he heard the post being delivered; then he limped quickly but quietly to the front door. Mr Pastry arrived there a moment afterwards and did a little perfunctory barking. Bernard held him by the collar with one hand while he sorted the various cards and letters with the other. There was a letter for him (he recognized the handwriting as that of the one ex-member of his original regiment with whom he still maintained some kind of touch), a letter, a small parcel and three cards for Marigold, two bills addressed to Adela, nothing for George, nothing for Shorty. He put one letter in his pocket, kept the other in his hand and left everything else on the hall table; then, after a hasty look to and fro, thrust the letter he held at Mr Pastry's snout.

'Come on, boy,' he whispered. 'Go for it. Come on. Kill it. Good God, *kill it*, you fool.'

After wagging his tail uncertainly for some seconds, the dog caught on to the new game, which indeed was straightforward enough, consisting as it did of tearing the letter to shreds with his teeth. It was quite a short game. When it was over, Bernard dismissed his playmate with a light kick in the rump and moved, no longer quietly, to Marigold's door, on which he knocked.

'Yes, who is it?' said a voice that might conceivably have come from a dedicated scientist in mid-experiment, or at least from such a character as shown in an old-fashioned film.

'Fuck you' was all Bernard said in reply, and he said it under his breath.

He found Marigold tying a piece of shiny green ribbon round a box-shaped object wrapped in shiny pink paper. She turned and looked up at him in understandable surprise.

'What brings you here?'

'It's that bloody dog of George's again, I'm afraid.' He spoke with great seriousness, with some inner concentration too: forming an alliance with Marigold was not a venture to be approached lightly. 'Look what I've just picked up by the front door.' He handed over the tatters of paper and went on talking. 'It really is too bad. In a sense, of course, I suppose one can't blame the creature, but it's hardly as if he's a puppy, is it? I'm afraid it looks as if he'll have to be—'

'Do you know who it's from?' Marigold's surprise had turned to something that closely resembled honest puzzlement.

'How should I know?'

'Well, it's addressed to you.'

'What?'

'I said it's addressed—'

'I meant I . . . Let me have a look.'

For the second time in two minutes Bernard recognized his friend's hand, and a part of his own name could still be made out on the remains of the envelope. By a great effort, he managed not to snatch from his pocket what he now knew must be Marigold's letter. 'You're quite right,' he said, so dizzy with rage that he put a hand on the corner of the dressing-table and knocked over a plastic bottle of baby oil. (What was she doing with *baby* oil?)

Her puzzlement gave way to suspicion. 'What made you think it was for me?'

'I didn't really, I don't know, I must have thought, after all you get more letters than anybody else, it probably might have been for you,' babbled Bernard, staring at a fragment of moist paper with *Note new address: The . . . shire* on it. Without volition he added, 'There was one for you anyway. I—'

'Where is it?'

'I . . .'

What with his leg and her speed off the mark, she was several paces ahead of him at the hall table, but by then he had the letter in his hand.

In a moment Marigold said, 'I can't find any letter here.'

As she spoke, Bernard entered on a strange evolution: backwards (to look under the table), downwards (to look further under the table) and forwards (to pick up anything that might have been lying under the table). He got to his feet again with some difficulty.

'Here it is. It must have slipped on to the floor.'

'But it wasn't there a moment ago.'

'It must have been. You didn't see it.'

'But I would have seen it if it had been there.'

'You didn't, however.' Bernard was trying to calm himself before he said anything more to compound his crassness. 'I had to bend down to see it.'

'But I'd have seen it while I was walking towards the table.'

'You might well have done, I agree. Nevertheless you failed to.'

'But it's all scrumpled up.'

'So it is.' It had had to be, to remain concealed in his hand. 'Not damaged to any material degree, though.'

'But how did it get like that?'

'I haven't the slightest idea. These things happen.'

'But why are you so upset?'

'I'm not upset, I'm just not used to sudden bending and stretching.'

'I think you got the dog to chew up what you thought was my letter and gave it your own by mistake.'

'Nonsense. Who on earth would do such an absurd thing?'

'An absurd man. A man like you.'

Marigold collected her correspondence and left him standing there.

Twenty-Five

That afternoon, Bernard was coming out of the lavatory (after a prolonged and painful session) just as Pusscat was passing. At the sight of him, she broke into a run towards the stairhead. He drew his pistol from its holster with the speed of, say, a middle-grade FBI trainee, followed, squeezed the trigger. A target moving directly away from a sharpshooter is almost as vulnerable as a stationary one: the jet of water found its mark in less than a second and never left it. Pusscat vanished in the direction of Marigold's room. A loud, repeated miaouing ensued. Bernard was just about to retreat towards his bedroom, with the idea of setting up a rough alibi, when he heard the approach of unsteady footsteps from the kitchen. As he peered down the stairs, he just caught a glimpse of Shorty with a soda-siphon in his hand; he too passed out of sight. A door opened. There was a brief mumble of voices, then Marigold's was raised.

'This cat is soaking wet.'

Shorty asked some question.

'I'll tell you how: by being squirted with that siphon. To think you—'

'I wouldn't do a thing like that, Marigold. I was only just taking it to the sitting-room for tomorrow. Anyway, look, you can see it's full. No, it isn't quite, is it? Well, these days you quite often—'

'Have you gone mad?'

'Not so's you'd notice.' Shorty too was beginning to sound quite angry. 'If you think I go round squirting cats you're the one that's mad.'

'How do you suggest she got in this state?'

'I don't suggest because I don't know and I've got no theories, Marigold. I'm sorry it's happened, but I had no hand in it, compree?'

'You're just like Bernard. It's not hard to see what drew the pair of you together.'

'You'd better be careful, Marigold, or you'll—'

'Are you threatening me?'

'Or you'll find yourself sinking to my level, and I'm sure you wouldn't care for that.'

There was a pause, followed by the slamming of one door and the shutting of another. Now Bernard did go to his bedroom, where he laughed till he cried.

Twenty-Six

At four-thirty the next morning, Christmas morning, Adela was wide awake. She had had a dream in which she was back at school, but retained her present age. None of the children, including somebody who was Marigold and yet did not look like Marigold, had taken any notice of her.

She knew from experience that her chance of any more sleep that night was poor. If a long and tiring day had not lain ahead of her, she would have filled in the time by reading; as it was, she decided she had better lie in the dark and rest. It should be easy enough: after all, there was plenty to look forward to in that day. Or rather, there ought to have been. But how was she to avoid continually remembering that, ten to one, this would be the last Christmas for which she would have Marigold's company? It was true that Marigold was given to saying one thing and doing another, or not doing anything, but she had sounded and looked unusually resolved when, last night, she said that Bernard's and Shorty's behaviour was intolerable and she had quite made up her mind to leave Tuppenny-hapenny Cottage as soon as her arrangements were completed, within the next fortnight if possible. Just what the respective bits of behaviour had been was obscure to Adela, not that that made the least difference: Marigold would not have listened to her attempts to mitigate or console, any more than

Bernard and Shorty would listen to her pleadings or reproaches; she could do nothing.

Adela tried to find a comfortable place on her pillow, which felt, as usual, like a small vegetable-sack stuffed with an assemblage of stoutly-constructed rag dolls. Not for the first time in her life, she wished she had been born with the ability to see when people meant what they said. Perhaps Marigold had no real intention of going after all. But the threat was there and cast a shadow.

What would she do if Marigold did go? Carry on, of course; no question about that. It was odd how straightforward, how almost easy, that was, even when there was nothing to carry on until. She remembered the end of the second war in Europe, how she had gone to bed on the night of the German surrender in some apprehension, wondering what it would feel like now that a great effort was finished and her small but all-absorbing part in it was finished too. And then, the next day, nothing seemed to have changed: there was always a job to do, and there always would be, with luck.

Abruptly, she sat up and put the light on. She could not just lie there waiting until it was time to go down and light the gas under the turkey. If she felt tired later in the day, she had only to leave Shorty in charge and slip upstairs for an hour's nap. But what was she going to do before and after seeing to the turkey? Well, afterwards she could go to Communion in the village. No; the experience would not uplift her, as it would once have done, merely leave her dejected and empty. Instead, what about making some fudge for the children? It would help to keep them quiet until tea if they did not care for the grown-up food in the middle of the day.

That touch of the practical finally got her going. She slipped along to and back from the bathroom and put on her man-made-fibre dress and short-sleeved jacket in navy blue with heavy touches of white, a costume settled upon after some thought the previous day. Soon she had her apron on too and was reviving the kitchen fire. It was not a cold morning – in an hour or so she would go out into the woods and watch and listen as the dawn came up. The fresh air would be invigorating and the experience itself – she had not been out of doors at daybreak for longer than she cared to remember – probably rather inspiring. Meanwhile, there was the fudge to do. Sugar, instant coffee, and condensed milk: Shorty's old-soldier tastes saw to it that there was plenty of that. Adela settled down to work.

Twenty-Seven

Some hours later, Bernard stood by the just-open door of his bedroom. He was unusually accoutred, with a damp washing-flannel slung across his face in the yashmak position – it was secured at the back of his head by a safety-pinned stretch of elastic purloined from Adela's work-box – a pair of bellows in one hand and a dustpan and brush in the other. On his bedside table, the radio was loudly relaying some carol or other. Marigold made her fleeting appearance. The nearby door duly shut and the key turned. Bernard moved into action.

He laid down his implements by the door in question and took from his pocket a small transparent sphere. This he placed as near as possible to the crack under the door, a chink measuring nearly a quarter of an inch, and crushed it noiselessly under the dustpan. At once a terrible and tremendous odour was released, so strong as to penetrate easily his improvised gas-mask. Retching almost continuously, he worked hard with the bellows to blow into the lavatory every possible molecule of vapour. He kept this up for twenty seconds or so, then rapidly and efficiently swept up the fragments.

A call came from George's bedroom down the landing. 'I say! Bernard, are you there? Bernard?'

'Coming.'

He was with George after a very short delay, his various tools safely hidden for the moment under Shorty's bed.

'I say, Bernard, what on earth is this frightful stink? Oh, merry Christmas, old boy.'

'Merry Christmas, George. I've no idea.'

'Could you open that window as wide as it'll go? It really is awful. What can it be?'

Bernard did as he was asked. 'Well . . . the only thing I can think of . . . I did happen to notice Marigold going into the bog.'

The left half of George's face expressed incredulity. 'But you don't mean . . . Surely no human . . . It's not like any ordinary . . .'

'Not ordinary, no. But she has been under the doctor. I suppose there may be something . . .'

'It smells to me like a stink-bomb.'

'Really? I don't think I've ever—'

'We used to muck about with them at school. Phew! Actually it is beginning to die down a bit.'

It had died down a good deal further by the time Marigold came into the room. She wished them a merry Christmas and kissed them both. It came natural to her to kiss George; Bernard she kissed partly because she hoped to shame him by doing so without the least hint of overt reluctance, partly because she knew he disliked being touched by anyone, and partly because the impending arrival of the young people made her feel generally benevolent.

'Funny smell in here,' she said, sniffing. 'I noticed it out there too.'

'Yes, we were wondering what it was,' said Bernard.

'I expect it's the drains. I'll tell Adela. Well, I must be on my way. See you downstairs soon, I hope, George.'

'Rum go, that,' said George when she had left. 'You'd have thought she'd have noticed it most when she was, well, closest to the drains. I think you can shut the window now, if you would.'

Bernard again obeyed. He did not try to speak. So much for his hopes of suggesting to Marigold that her insides had started to decompose! The patent and total failure of Operation Stink was mainly due to two factors unknown to him. He had not risked an indoor trial, and his outdoor one, while useful in establishing the fragility of the capsules, had told him nothing of the speed with which their contents were dispersed; thus only a small fraction of the gas had ever got into the lavatory. And that small fraction had been promptly blown out again by the draught from its window, which the fastidious Marigold invariably threw open on arrival there.

Bernard's Christmas was off to a bad start.

Twenty-Eight

'Now it's for the client to decide. We're running a full presentation in the first week of January,' said Keith MacKelvie to Marigold. He was twenty-nine and, so she understood, being more and more successful in something to do with advertisements. By his side, held rather tightly by the wrist, stood Finn, his five-year-old son; a yard away was Keith's wife, Finn's mother and Marigold's granddaughter, Rachel, who was twenty-six and was holding, also by the wrist and a little more tightly, Vanessa MacKelvie, aged nearly four. Adela and Bernard were within earshot. The group was standing between the piano and the sitting-room window, where there was a view of the rock-garden with iris and narcissus in flower. To one side stood a large mountain ash with a great many berries on it, and the woods stretched beyond. In the moments of sunshine, bright for the time of year, it was a pleasant outlook. A total stranger paying a call of not more than thirty seconds' duration might quite well, thought Keith to himself, mistake the house for a tolerable place to live.

'I see,' said Marigold, nodding hard. 'That's the man who . . . What does he do, Keith?'

'He makes pet food.'

'What?' asked Bernard.

'He makes pet food.'

Surely not all those nearby, including the children, could in fact have spoken as one, but it seemed very like it to Bernard. '*Pet food*,' he said, conveying reluctance to believe that anyone who enjoyed rights of entry to the house should have to do with such a monster.

'Yes, pet food.' Keith, as well as having started to detest Bernard on sight, several years before, had not gone far and fast in his profession by accident, without, that is, the aid of a quick insight into others. 'The main ones,' he went on as slowly as he dared, 'are Bow-Wow and Mew. They're for dogs and cats' – pause – 'respectively. Then . . . of course . . . there's the stuff they call . . . Chirrup.'

'That's for budgies,' said Finn.

'*Budgies.*'

'Budgerigars,' said Keith sonorously, then speeded up. 'Small cage-birds, very popular with the—'

'I know. I know what they are.'

'Is it a big firm?' asked Marigold.

'Enormous. Quite e-nor-mous. The chief shag must be a million-aire several times over. Came here from Hungary in 1956 without a penny. I must say I admire a chap like that. He's Jewish, as you might expect.' This last Keith knew to be untrue, but, with justifiable confidence, he had inferred that Bernard was anti-semitic. 'They're brilliant at making money.'

'Indeed they are,' said Bernard in a high monotone.

'And at playing the violin and the piano and things like that,' said Adela quickly. 'I mean the Jews are brilliant at that too. They're very artistic. We mustn't forget that.'

'Mustn't we?'

'And you're making up all this man's advertisements for him, Keith,' said Marigold.

'No, I'm only to do with Bow-Wow. I'm in charge of—'

'Is it good?' asked Adela. 'I was thinking Mr Pastry might like it.'

'Mr . . . ? Oh—' Keith managed to suppress the blasphemy that sprang to his lips as he remembered who Mr Pastry was. 'Er, yes, he probably would. I've had many a worse portion of tinned meat than Bow-Wow. They sell a—'

'You mean you've *tasted* it?' asked Marigold.

'Yes, they have what they call quality testing sessions where it's made, and you're expected to join in if you happen to be there. The thing to do is keep to the Bow-Wow side of the room. Mew's worth steering clear of unless you're a cat. Chirrup's not bad if you don't mind a mouthful of seeds and gravel. Yes, they take a lot of—'

'You've *eaten* a *dog* food?' Marigold was exchanging glances of unabated shock, horror, outrage and so forth with Adela.

'Yes,' muttered Keith, muttered that he might not bawl at the top of his voice. 'It's got to be fit for human consumption, you see, which is why—'

'But who would eat it?' asked Adela. 'For an actual meal, I mean.'

'I suppose the blackle-packles might,' said Marigold.

Keith had been on general alert all along, and he made not the least sound or facial movement; it was Finn who staggered and nearly fell.

'Stand still, Finn.'

'I was. You pulled me.'

'Be quiet. Yes, Goldie, very badly-paid people might eat Bow-Wow, and they wouldn't come to any—'

'But why can't they just say it's unfit for human consumption?'

'Well, then a lot of people wouldn't give it to their dogs.'

'No doubt,' said Bernard, and turned away.

Keith was seized by boredom – a poor word for the consuming, majestic sensation that engulfed him, comparable in intensity to a once-in-a-lifetime musical experience, or what would be felt by the average passenger in a car driven by a drunk man late for an appointment. Needling Bernard had given temporary relief, the couple of minutes a member of a forced-labour gang might spend leaning on his spade. All too soon, the overseer was back with his whip. Rachel took the now writhing children off to do a jigsaw puzzle, or watch while she did it. He could not blame her; not all that far from crying (the fellow who coined 'bored to tears' would have made a fortune in the slogan-writing game), Keith led the two old women through a sort of explanation of how television commercials were put together, an explanation preceded by an explanation, for Adela's benefit, of what a television commercial was.

After a week or so, Marigold said, 'So this advertisement you've done, they're going to put it on the television.'

'That's what I hope. I've got the brands manager, the, one of the important blokes behind me. Now it's up to the marketing director, the, an even more important bloke.'

'And he has to see it, privately,' said Marigold with deliberation, 'and decide whether he likes it, and if he does like it, then, then they'll put it on the television, and you'll have succeeded.'

'That's it!' Keith's despair waned for a moment.

'And when is this happening, this private . . . show?'

'The first week in January.'

'Now Trevor, *Keith*, you're to telephone me as soon as you know the result. I insist on being told straight away. Promise me.'

'All right, Goldie,' said Keith, deciding that at the same time he had better inform President Allende, who must have quite as much at stake in the matter of the Bow-Wow commercial as Marigold had. He added with a vague sense of precaution, though quite truthfully, 'I've sometimes had trouble getting through to here.'

Adela looked puzzled for a moment. 'Getting through? Oh, you mean on the telephone. That's me, I'm afraid. Or it might have been me. Once I forgot to pay the bill and they cut us off. No, twice. I must try to—'

'It's not surprising you forget something once in a way,' said Marigold, smiling with her head on one side, 'considering how much you have to remember. Adela runs the whole show here, you know, Keith. She does a marvellous job.'

'I'm sure she does.'

'Oh, I only—'

'She pampers me in the most outrageous way. I don't deserve it the least little bit. She won't let me lift a finger, will you, Adela? Mind you, I'm such a wash-out I couldn't be trusted to boil an egg.'

Adela's red face had turned a deeper red. Her Christmas was made, whatever might be going to be unmade. In a little while she moved off, to let Marigold have Keith to herself, and joined Rachel and the children, not pushing herself forward, just sitting near them on her tapestry chair in case they wanted her to join in. Vanessa turned and stared at her thoughtfully for a quarter of a minute or so before staring at her mother with an expression that told of some question, or entreaty, not quite brought to the point of speech. Finn had not had to turn in order to stare thoughtfully at Adela, who went over to the Louis Quinze area. Here George, propped on the sofa, was telling Trevor and Tracy that Communism was a system founded on fear.

'I couldn't agree more, George,' said Trevor, wishing he knew how to show in full his inability to agree more.

'Absolutely diabolical,' said Tracy.

'Diabolical is the exact word. In 1921—'

At this point, Shorty, who had been seeing to drinks, bustled up and, swaying hardly at all, said,

'Couple of carols, Adela? I think the kids might like 'em.'

'Not more than two, Shorty, and not more than, say, four verses. Then we really ought to have the presents, because we don't want to—'

'I'm right up there with you, Adela.' He was not best pleased at the implication that having carols on Christmas morning was a tiresome and eccentric indulgence of his own. 'If the carols go on too long, that holds up handing out the presents, and holding up handing out the presents means holding up lunch-on, and holding up lunch-on's bad.'

'But surely it's Christmas dinner, isn't it?' asked George. 'I mean, the main meal's usually—'

'So it is, George, so it is. Once more hath Shorty erred.'

After calling for silence in the manner first of someone imitating a sergeant-major quite well, and then of someone imitating an Oberstürmbannführer almost as well, Shorty introduced the idea of carols in a pan-American accent. He sat down at his piano, played (not too badly) a few bars of *Alexander's Ragtime Band*, apologized, and went into *While Shepherds Watched*. By the end of the first verse, most people were singing, or at least la-la-ing to the tune.

Trevor took in the home-made paper-chains that, falsifying George's prediction that there would be no you stretch them from one corner to the other, met at the partly-intact electrolier at the middle of the room, the holly arranged along the mantelshelf and round the stained oval mirror above it, the Christmas tree (dug up, no doubt, in the woods by Shorty) hung with artificial frost and coloured tin spheres, the pile of variegated parcels and packets at its foot: Adela's planning and her and Shorty's work. A lot of work, done for much less effect. Of eleven people in the room, perhaps two, Adela and George, would positively enjoy the display, two more, Finn and Vanessa, would notice it in full for about half a minute, and another, Marigold, could have been counted on to complain if there had been none. And that was that. Did Adela know of the disparity between her intentions and their results? It made no difference either way: the thought was what counted, and she had simply done what had had to be done. That did not mean that doing as much was negligible or ridiculous or hypocritical.

Tracy saw the same incongruities as Trevor, but they brought to her mind a selection of fairly uncomplicated ironies about good cheer and the festive season, and she felt nothing much more than a mild, inert repulsion.

Keith was not interested in any of that. He threw himself into the singing with as much gusto as he could, short of obvious parody, also with the hope of seeming in retrospect to have enjoyed the day in some part, and was grateful too for another unexpected few minutes' worth of leaning on his spade.

Rachel was fully contented: the children were behaving well, and someone other than herself was doing all the cooking for the whole day.

While Shepherds Watched came to an end with a florid run on the piano not much disfigured by wrong notes. Shorty was having a fine time – bar getting pissed (and he was doing that too) he liked nothing better than a good old sing-song, and here was the chance of one, a rarity in this household. Now he started on *O Come, All Ye Faithful*.

'. . . Joyful and triumphant,' he sang, and continued at a safe volume, 'The Queen was in the parlour, dopping bread and honey. The maid was in the garden . . .' He caught sight of Marigold on her knees between her great-grandchildren, an arm round the restive shoulders of each. The bitch was singing away fit to bust; not only that, but in a way that made out that she had seen to it herself that everybody was having a rare old treat. 'Then along came a bloody great shitehawk,' sang Shorty, slowing down the tempo, 'and chomped . . . off . . . her nose.'

After that they had the presents. Those from the guests to the hosts were chiefly a disguised dole: tins or pots of more or less luxurious food, bottles of hard liquor, wide-spectrum gift tokens. Hosts showered guests with diversely unwearable articles of clothing: to Keith from Adela, a striped necktie useful for garrotting underbred rivals in his trade; to Tracy from George, a liberation-front lesbian's plastic apron. Under a largely unspoken kind of non-aggression pact, the guests gave one another things like small boxes of chocolates or very large boxes of matches with (say) aerial panoramas of Manhattan on their outsides and containing actual matches each long enough, once struck, to kindle the cigarettes of (say) the entire crew of a fair-sized merchant vessel, given the assembly of that crew in some relatively confined space. Intramural gifts included a bathroom sponge, a set of saucepans, a cushion in a lop-sided cover, a photograph-frame wrought by some vanished hand and with no photograph in it, an embroidered knitting-bag. Keith watched carefully what Bernard gave, half expecting a chestnut-coloured wig destined for Adela, or a lavishly-illustrated book on karate for George, but was disappointed, though he savoured Bernard's impersonation of a man going all out to hide his despondency as he took the wrappings off present after useless, insultingly cheap, no doubt intended to be facetious, present.

Twenty-Nine

'Do you think, er,' said Keith, '. . . do you think they spend *all* their time thinking about it or merely nearly all their time?'

'Quite possibly not as much time as all that,' answered Trevor, urinating as he spoke, for the two stood now in the upstairs lavatory. 'If you live with something, you may end up with it not meaning as much to you as if it only turned up now and then. You know, like background noise.'

'Like who was that bugger in mythology that the grapes were always swinging up out of reach and the stream sank whenever he bent down and tried to drink out of it? Pretty noisy sort of noise at their time of life. Tantalus. He'd have noticed being hungry and thirsty a bit as the days went by. More like foreground noise. Aircraft noise when you're living twenty yards from Heathrow only moving closer.'

'Are you pissed?'

'Yes.' Keith replaced Trevor at the w.c. 'Do you know that SF story where the space pilots or something do six hours on and six months off because it's so shagging? Cordwainer Smith, that's right. I thought he was overdoing it rather until I turned up here today. You know my father was sixty last month? Coming along nicely. I suppose with luck we might get a couple of weeks between the last of them going and us being in their situation. And if you're not pissed you must be out of your mind. This is the last time I do this.'

'So you always say round about now. You'll be here next time.'

'Because of thinking what a bloody good chap I am when it's all over. Sudden burst of self-admiration.'

'And non-sudden trickles of thinking you're a shit for not coming.'

'Oh, they've got us there. Because we know how much better off we are.'

'We'd better go down. Isn't it marvellous, having a wife?'

'Yeah,' said Keith. 'And being able to finish a sentence.'

'We'll be just the same when we get to their age.'

'Oh no we won't. Horrible, yes. Boring, sure. But not like them. Chummy little crowd, aren't they? And I take it back about us being boring. Boring on that scale, anyhow.'

'I'd like to have a tape of what they were saying about their grand-parents and so on thirty years ago. Come on.'

'Would you? Off sharp at ten, Trev. A mere eight-plus hours. Unless one of them checks out before then. Two or three of them check out.'

Thirty

Christmas dinner was something of a success; it passed off, at any rate, without bloodshed. Marigold, with the young in close attendance, actually enjoyed herself, not least because Finn and Vanessa paid so much attention to her. (On the journey down, their father had several times ordered them to behave in this way, adding far from casually that, according to rumours he had not yet been able to check, very naughty and disobedient children were sometimes made into Bow-Wow.) George was happy too, and explained to any adult not in mid-phrase that many traditional features of Christmas were of pagan origin, that there was no reason to suppose that there were not intelligent beings on worlds other than our own, and similar matters. Bernard said little; he was trying to reconcile his dislike of Trevor for having a lot of hair on his face with his dislike of Keith for having none, and found the task difficult until it dawned on him that of course Trevor was flaunting the fact that he was young while Keith was trying to pretend he was no different from anyone else. Adela was too concerned that everything should go well to derive much active pleasure from the occasion, but now and again she was warmed by the memory of what Marigold had said about the running of the household. Shorty, what with the normal covert drinking and abnormal overt drinking he had done, was drunk, and, after breaking one glass and upsetting another full of wine, fell sound asleep at table.

Thirty-One

By pre-arrangement, the Fishwicks and MacKelvies insisted in unison that the kitchen should be left as it was until coffee, liqueurs, cigars and other treats had been consumed in the sitting-room, at which stage the four of them would do all the washing- and clearing-up – it looked kind and, as Keith had put it to Trevor, was preferable to going fifteen rounds with Muhammad Ali, which in turn, so he suggested, would have been preferable to an extra half-hour with the oldsters.

The quadripartite insistence proved effective. Full of food and fudge, virtually force-fed by their parents to the point of stupefaction, Finn and Vanessa were encouraged without trouble to have a prolonged nap in their great-grandmother's room. Bernard was sincerely sorry to see them go. With all his heart, he had hoped that one or both of them would commit some salient piece of misbehaviour: pissing on this, shitting on that, being sick over the other. Their temporary departure did not, of course, rule out such joyful possibilities, but it did postpone them, substantially reduce the period within which they might be made actual.

When the five full-time occupants of Tuppenny-hapenny Cottage were settled together in the sitting-room (an extraordinary state of affairs), George drew luxuriously on his second cigar of the day and said,

'Well, I don't know about the rest of you, but I've had the finest Christmas present I could possibly have wished for.'

Shorty roused himself, no mean feat after the MacKelvie-provided shot of green Chartreuse and the Fishwick-provided shot of Bénédictine he had thrown down on top of everything else. 'What's that, George?'

'Let me put it this way. I've been given a bottle of after-shave lotion, a pullover, two pairs of socks, a potted plant to stick on my bedside table, a pair of slippers and various other very kind gifts I could name. What does that suggest to you?'

'Well, you seem to have done pretty well, George.'

'Indeed I have, and I'm most grateful to all concerned, but that's not what I'm driving at. Surely one of you must see.'

'You've had a lot of nice presents,' said Adela.

'Oh yes, but . . . Hasn't anybody noticed anything?'

'Let's have it, George,' said Shorty.

'I know what they're all called. I can put a name to them. I can name pretty well everything.' George pointed at various objects in the room. 'Clock, piano, ashtray, sofa, glove, table, rocking-chair, bookcase, statuette, bowl, picture, another picture, and I could go on, but I don't need to. You must remember how for a long time I couldn't think what things were called because of my stroke, and the doctor said it might or might not get better of its own accord? Well, it's got better. It could have happened – I can't say when. Not overnight, I imagine. But I'd got into the habit of using periphrases for the names of things, phrases that more or less meant the same, so as not to have to keep hesitating and talking tripe. As a result I stopped worrying about not being able to think of the names; I don't know whether that's got anything to do with it. Anyhow, it dawned on me just today. You've no idea how marvellous it feels. I don't mind being half paralysed now, except that it's a nuisance to other people. The gift of language is a very precious thing. After all, it's what differentiates us from the animal kingdom. It's the most human—'

'Which means that in future,' said Bernard with a smile, 'you'll be able to bore us all even more efficiently than in the past.'

'If you'll pardon the intrusion, Bernard, I don't think that's very funny,' said Shorty.

His tone was mild; Bernard's was not when he answered, a notable departure from his usual practice of confining acrimony to the content of what he said. 'Since when have we been expected to regard you as an authority on what is and what is not funny?'

'Since never, Bernard,' said Shorty, laying the mildness on as thick as any man could. 'I probably know nothing at all about that. But perhaps I do know a bit about what is and what is not a nice thing to say. Good taste's what it used to be called.'

'So now you're an authority on good taste.' Bernard was trying hard to lower his voice and force the smile back on to his face. 'I'm bound to say I find that an equally remarkable concept. What other treasures of authoritativeness have you in your store? What clothes to wear? How to stay sober?'

'Here, I say, you fellows,' began George.

'Please, both of you,' said Adela with as much urgency as she could convey, 'don't let's be like that. It is Christmas, after all.'

'So it is, upon my word.' By now, Bernard was in relative control of himself. 'I knew there must be some explanation.'

Adela glanced at Marigold to see how she was responding to this interchange, and what she saw, to her surprise, was that Marigold was not responding at all, had evidently not so much as taken it in. She had not (now Adela came to think of it) said a word or made any sort of move since the young people had left the room.

At a second attempt, Shorty rose to his feet. 'I think, if you'll excuse me, Adela and Marigold and George, I'll betake myself to my chaste couch, there to enjoy a spell of blanket-bashing of indefinite duration.'

'Oh, don't go, old boy,' said George. 'Stay and have another spot of port or brandy.'

'Thank you, George, but I fear lest that might prove unwise. In the language of the Hun, au revoir.'

As soon as Shorty was out of the room, Bernard said to George with an air of concern, 'I hope I didn't offend you by what I said a few moments ago. I was only—'

'Bernard, you couldn't offend me today if you tried. And of course

I knew you were joking. A chap would have to have a pretty poor sense of humour not to see that.'

'I think possibly I was a bit hard on Shorty just now. I'd better drop him a word of apology later.'

'A sense of humour is important in all sorts of ways,' said George, and went on to outline some of them to Bernard.

'What's wrong, dear?' asked Adela quietly.

Marigold looked up and hugged her elbows to her sides. 'Nothing. I've just come to a decision.'

'Oh, Marigold . . .' Adela clasped her short-fingered hands together. Why was it that other people's decisions always turned out badly for her?

'I've changed my mind. I'm not leaving here. I'll never leave.'

'Oh, darling, I am so glad,' said Adela, successfully struggling not to embrace the other woman. 'So very glad. But . . . has something awful happened that's made you change your mind? You seem all . . .'

'Nothing's happened.'

This was true in a restricted sense. Half an hour earlier, Trevor had recalled to her the Christmas of five years previously, when her husband had been alive and in full vigour, had indeed entertained the company with anecdotes about comic disasters that had befallen him during his career as a glass merchant. Or rather, the boy had failed to recall any single fact or detail to her: she had forgotten the entire occasion and it stayed forgotten. Searching introspection had since told her something of how much else she had forgotten. Marigold had loved her husband for forty-eight years; so, at any rate, she would have said, and would have meant it. Now she could not remember their first meeting, their engagement, their wedding, their first house, what clothes he used to wear, what sort of voice he had had, what he had looked like – she had photographs by the score, and she had slipped into her room to turn them through, but to see what he had looked like was not the same as remembering. It was as if he and their life together had been taken away from her. At least Adela had known him, Bernard and Shorty had met him often, several times, more than once. While she stayed with them and could talk to them about him, he would not be altogether obliterated, not unless or until her mind became unfit to grasp the fact of his former existence. It no longer mattered that the others would witness at close quarters the advance of her senility.

Tracy, Trevor and Keith came in before anything else was said. (Rachel was in Marigold's room, officially to keep the children quiet, though they needed no such attention, being sound asleep, and she was herself sound asleep, her favourite state since Finn's birth.) Tracy immediately sensed that something or other was going on between the two older women, decided with as little delay that it was none of her business, moved across to the two older men, and was surprised to see a welcoming expression on Bernard's face; she could not have known how close he had come to going for George with the poker.

'I was just saying to Bernard here that a sense of humour is more precious than pearls or rubies or any number of motor-cars or luxury yachts or private aeroplanes or castles,' said George, in whom the full restoration of vocabulary, on top of a few drinks and some natural loquaciousness, was producing a florid, almost aureate style of talk.

'Yes,' said Tracy. She thought for a moment and added, 'Yes.'

'I mean to say, supposing you do eat off silver plate with a pearl-handled knife and fork and drink your wine out of cut glass . . .' After listing further concrete signs of affluence, George went on to question their real worth to anybody without a sense of humour.

Like Tracy, Trevor had noticed the tension on the other side of the room, but he made towards it, walking however with very short strides of not more than eighteen inches or so. The effect of this was almost to double the time it took him to reach the old ladies while giving the impression, from where they sat, that his gait was quite normal. He used the seconds thus won to push words through his mind as fast as possible. They can't help it (he gabbled silently) they've got nothing to look forward to it's just got to be accepted you'll be like it yourself one day you'll be out of here soon oh Christ. Aloud, he said,

'Well, that's all seen to. Everything, er, seen to.'

'Trevor, darling,' said Marigold: 'it was such fun remembering that Christmas. I was thinking about the one before that. We did spend it at home, didn't we? Or were we—?'

'No, that was the year you and Grandpop went to that hotel in Eastbourne and we all drove down on Christmas Day.'

'Oh yes.'

It was obvious to Trevor that his grandmother had forgotten the whole thing, which should be no surprise, considering her age. Well, he would find it less of a chore to give her an obsessively detailed account of the occasion than to try to converse with her. 'The moment we arrived Grandpop ordered a magnum of champagne and you said it was extravagant of him . . .'

Unconscious of anything amiss, Keith had gone straight to one of the tapestry chairs beyond the fireplace carrying a large dictionary (the property of George) and a note-pad. He now began to look for rare words and to record their definitions for later use in the promised game of Call My Bluff, a task he would pursue with the most thorough and prolonged care, prolonged at any rate until pity for Trevor and Tracy should quite overwhelm him.

Bernard gave a small start, as if at the memory of something over-looked, and left the room at a fair pace.

'I must see to the children's tea in a few minutes,' said Adela.

Thirty-Two

The plan was simple in outline, but there was a particular detail which would call for the utmost vigilance; one must be grateful, on the other hand, that it had been foreseen in good time. Alone in the kitchen, Bernard looked through the rubbish-container until he found an empty tomato-purée tin. It was small for his purpose; still, it would have to do. He rinsed it thoroughly under the tap, hurried into the outside lavatory and so arranged matters there that when he returned he was carrying perhaps five fluid ounces of urine. Now came the dangerous part of the operation. To light the gas and put the tin on the flame was the work of a moment; to stand by, as always, called for resolution. Just when the contents, as a dipped finger-tip showed, had reached the estimated necessary temperature (not low, in view of the coldness of the house and the notorious rapidity with which small bodies of liquid lose their heat), Bernard heard Adela's step in the hallway. He snapped off the gas and picked up the tin, the outside of which proved unexpectedly hot, but the aid of handkerchief or kettle-holder was excluded. Wincing slightly with pain, he juggled the tin from hand to hand behind his back and waited for his sister to come into the kitchen. She would not: she stood in the doorway turning her broad face to and fro and beaming.

'They've made a lovely job of it, haven't they? Draining-board scrubbed down and the tea-cloths hung up to dry. They are so sweet, those four.'

'Oh, enchanting.'

'I really do believe you're enjoying Christmas.'

'To some extent.'

'Marigold has decided to stay with us after all.'

'Has she?'

'It means such a lot to me.'

'I know.'

How much longer was he to go on chatting away with a can of piss about his person? Still Adela did not move; he was positive she had consciously noticed nothing out of the way, but her instinct for obstruction ran deep and wide. He was on the point of stepping forward himself when he realized that he dared not risk a jostle on the cramped threshold.

'I've got to do the children's tea,' said Adela, 'because they soon get hungry at that age, and it's not fair to keep them waiting, and poor Rachel has enough to do every other day of the year.'

'I can find no fault with your reasoning.'

He held the container now in one hand, fingers pointed downwards round it in a grip that would hide it from most eyes; its smallness had become an asset. At last Adela came right into the room. She sniffed the air.

'Funny smell, isn't there?'

'I haven't noticed anything.'

'Perhaps one of the animals . . .'

'Very likely.'

He was away and into the hall, and was there instantly blocked again by Rachel and her offspring grouped in arrow-head formation between him and the stairs. He noticed scarves, gloves, a woolly hat or so. He said without premeditation,

'I thought you were supposed to be having tea.'

'Walkies first,' said Rachel, 'while Auntie Adela gets the tea ready. Then we all come back and eat it round the fire and have a lovely time.'

She spoke as if she thought this conversational style the most suitable for Bernard as well as for the children. Or so it seemed to him at that moment. Before he could be let past, or ask to be, he saw that Finn's attention was caught: the child's head was just at the right/wrong level.

'What's that thing you've got there in your hand?'

'It smells funny,' said Vanessa, craning forward.

'It's nothing. Kindly allow me—'

'It smells like—'

'Be quiet, you two,' said Rachel, 'and get out of Uncle Bernard's way.'

'But,' said Finn, 'it's like, you know, when you—'

'It's somebody's—'

'It's special medicine for my bad leg. Now . . .'

At last he was through and on the way upstairs, leaving behind him an excited altercation in childish whispers and stern adult undertones. He paused in the first-floor lavatory to regain his composure and to tell himself that a lighter man might well have been deflected from his purpose by such hazards – tell himself so only briefly, for time was now vital.

Behind the screen in the bedroom, Shorty was asleep with such extravagant soundness as to suggest a drunken gaoler in a farce impersonated by someone given to play-acting much more than to acting: Shorty himself, for instance. With quick deft movements, Bernard twitched aside the incongruously clean blankets and poured the urine over the crotch of Shorty's trousers. He did not stir, much less wake, as (Bernard had reasoned) he might well have done if the liquid had been perceptibly below blood heat. Bernard put the blankets back and stared down at the sleeper.

'If you'll pardon the intrusion, Shorty, I think that's very funny,'
he said, and left the room.

Thirty-Three

Half an hour later, Shorty drifted back to a waking state. He became
aware by degrees of a dampness, here and there a wetness, in his lower
clothing.

'*Huh*-lo-ullo-ullo, what's all this ere?' he said. 'Pissed myself, eh?
Well, it won't be the first time, nor the last, I hope, thanks very much.
Funny in a way, choking for a piss after you've just pissed yourself.
Goes to show how much one can imbibe without its being fully clear
to one how much one has imbibed, my lords, ladies and gentlemen,
ra-ra-ra. Pooh, stinko!'

He very quickly established that the spillage had not extended to
any of his bedclothes, went into the lavatory and made water for a
couple of minutes, had a prolonged bath during which he also washed
his trousers and underpants, got outside a toothglassful of Dr Macdonald's while he dressed, and arrived downstairs in excellent condition:
the very picture, in fact, of a man untroubled by the least fear of losing
or having begun to lose control of his bodily functions.

Operation Incontinence had gone the way of Operation Stink.

Thirty-Four

'Nemel,' said George, 'is an Arab sweetmeat or dessert made of dates,
poppy seeds, coriander seeds, peppermint, rose petals and gum traga-
canth, mixed with a pestle in a mortar, served in earthenware cups
and decorated with cactus flowers and the feathers of the bulbul or
Eastern nightingale.'

'Rubbish,' said Bernard amiably. 'To start with, it's *a* nemel. A
nemel is a pompous old windbag head over heels in love with the

sound of his own voice and consumed by a desire to show off his fund of trivial and boring information.' He paused, then added, 'So called after the character le Sieur de Némel in Molière's *Le Misanthrope*.'

Adela peered through her spectacles at the slip of paper on her lap. 'Er, nemel,' she said in some puzzlement, 'is just to name, verb. To name.'

'I simply don't understand,' said Marigold from her Louis Quinze sofa on the opposite side of the sitting-room fireplace. 'To name verb? What does it mean, darling?'

Trevor, next to her, spoke up quickly. 'It must mean like, when I have a son I'm going to nemel him Joe, instead of name him Joe. That's right, isn't it, Adela?'

'Yes. Yes, that's right.'

'Fine, thanks. Now . . .' Trevor turned successively to Marigold and Tracy. 'I say it's George.'

'But it must be Adela,' said his grandmother, fitting a cigarette into her shagreen holder. 'Surely that's obvious.'

'Ah, that's what we're supposed to think.'

'But surely you could see, Keith dear . . . *Trevor* dear. She was just reading it off that piece of paper.' Marigold had not lowered her voice at all.

'That's just it,' murmured Trevor. 'Double bluff, you see.'

'But a thing like that would never occur to her,' said Marigold at the same pitch as before.

'Well, I pick George.' Trevor looked at his wife and made the pupils of his eyes vibrate in a disturbing way that was an established domestic signal. 'What do you think, Tracy?'

'George.'

'Right, that's two George, one Adela. How did we do?'

'And the teller of the truth was . . . ?' asked Keith from the rocking-chair.

After some hesitation, Adela raised her hand.

'I *told* you, you noodle-poodles.'

'*One* only to Goldie's team. Well done, Adela, well done, George.'

With a flourish, Keith made an entry on his pad. After eight hours of pretty continuous fire, it was wonderful to be merely in the frying-pan. It seemed that everybody had now mastered the complexity and strangeness of a game wherein two members of a team improvised false definitions of some piece of lexical slag and the third (appointed in advance and in secret by that team's captain) offered the true one; mastered, also, the scoring system whereby a correct guess at the truth-teller's identity obtained one point for the opposing team, an incorrect guess none at all – and that these points were cumulative, issuing, after a time previously agreed, in a result. That time was now only a matter of minutes away.

(In the next room, Marigold's room, Rachel was minding the children. This meant in practice that she slept in a rather knobbly easy-chair with an abandonment almost approaching that of Shorty's drunken-gaoler performance, while each of them, in strict rotation, and in something near total silence, climbed on to the bed and aimed one gob of spittle at the open mouth of the other, stretched out on the floor immediately beneath. As with their elders' game, there was a scoring system here, but it was observed with less rigour: a direct hit, at any rate a total direct hit, was less easy to establish.)

Keith announced the score so far, then said, 'I suggest we have a team change. Good old Shorty's been seeing to coffee and drinks and making up the fire and generally looking after us. I think we ought to give him a turn at the game, eh, Shorty?'

'Grassy-arse, seen yours. Delighted to oblige.'

'I wonder if . . .' Keith pretended to consider. 'Tracy, would you mind dropping out?'

'No, er, of course not.'

Shorty sat down next to Marigold, who moved up for him a little further than necessary. Keith handed Trevor three folded slips.

'And the next word is spronk, s,p,r,o,n,k. Spronk.'

There was a timed pause for consideration, part of which Shorty used for very deliberately topping up his glass of Bénédictine.

'Spronk is a dialect word,' said Trevor, throwing himself about on his chair to imply desperate improvisation, 'meaning a shoot or, er, a sprout, or . . . the stump of a tree or of a tooth, or it used to mean, er, a spark, yes, a spark. It's a very rare word and has pretty well died out these days.'

Marigold gazed at her slip. 'A spronk is a man who hates everybody and whose only pleasure in life is being sarcastic to people and trying to make them as unhappy as he is. A very lazy man too. Named after Hezekiah Spronk in . . . one of Dickens's books.'

'A splonk,' said Shorty, 'or rather *to* splonk is to have a bloody good time boozing away like the hammers of hell. In the words of the poet, let us eat, splonk and be merry. Hic.'

Bernard's team was divided in its response, he himself opting for Trevor, George for Shorty and Adela for Marigold. Again, one point scored. Trevor said to Keith,

'Shall we play something else? I think this is getting a bit, you know, sort of dull.'

'Do you? *I* think it's fascinating. Anyway, there must be one more round to even things up. Each team has got to have the same number of goes, you see. The next word is . . . jimp, j,i,m,p. Jimp.'

'A jimp is an abbreviation for a chimpanzee,' said Adela. 'Some people say chimp, of course, but not everybody. Some of them say jimp instead.'

'To jimp,' said Bernard, looking into the fire, 'is to behave in an exaggeratedly theatrical way in order to conceal the fact that nothing whatsoever is taking place inside one's head. Or, transitively, to jimp *somebody* is to make him, or her, do everything for one while patronizing and humiliating him, or her.'

Before Bernard had quite finished, Shorty leaned over sideways and seemed not so much to spill as to pour a couple of ounces of Bénédictine on to the skirt of Marigold's dress. Trevor immediately started wondering whether this move was an additional assault on his grandmother, a diversion designed to prevent her from, say, scratching Bernard's eyes out (very much on the cards an instant earlier), or a drunken accident, but he had to stop wondering quite as soon when she in turn behaved in a way equally hard to evaluate. But, either as the result of a delayed reflex of recoil, or by way of an actual blow in retaliation, her elbow came up and caught Shorty hard under the chin. He was still off balance and fell sideways in the opposite direction, over the end of the sofa and half into the fireplace, his head near the fire itself. A moment later Adela also crashed to the ground, having tripped up over her own feet on her way to assist Shorty. Keith soon pulled him out of harm's way; Trevor helped Adela up; both the fallen seemed undamaged. At that stage, Marigold, who had risen to her feet, collapsed backwards on to the sofa. Tracy ran to her.

'I think she's fainted. Could someone get a glass of water?'

Trevor did, and quite soon Marigold opened her eyes.

'I'm all right,' she said. At no point had she been other than all right, though just now as angry – with Bernard – as she had ever been in her life. Her mind, whatever its defects, had worked fast enough to suggest to her that to throw a faint would be an unimprovable way to avoid having to apologize to Shorty (whom she had meant to jostle or possibly thump, not set fire to), would make her the focus of attention and solicitude, and might also suggest to Bernard that any effect of his insults on her had been erased by the scene that had happened to follow them. That would have to do for the time being.

Trevor turned to Keith. 'Get the kids up and ready to move and we'll put her to bed.'

'Shall I ring the doctor?' asked Bernard in an anxious tone.

'No thank you.'

'Sorry about the dress, Marigold,' said Shorty, who had fully intended to souse her in Bénédictine, but had been too drunk to make the action look drunken. 'I'm none the worse myself, you'll be glad to hear.'

Adela knelt by the sofa and began swabbing at the stained skirt with her handkerchief.

Tracy caught Bernard's eye and at once looked away. With her back to the windows, she had had a good view of the events of the last minute. When Shorty fell, there had been a general reaction; even George had clearly done all he could to get up, out of instinct. Only Bernard had not moved at all. Could he really have been indifferent to the sort of thing that might quite easily have been going to happen to his old boy-friend? She felt for a cigarette and looked at her watch.

Thirty-Five

It was Adela who, in the face of Marigold's renewed assurances that she was all right, telephoned Dr Mainwaring on the morning after Boxing Day. Two more days passed before he could, or would, come, but come he did about the middle of the morning, when Adela was out at the shops.

As before, Marigold had arrayed herself with some care for his visit: second-best trouser-suit, blue-and-green-striped shirt with high long-pointed collar, queen-sized cameo brooch, cigarette-holder at the ready. Besides routine motives like putting up a show of not giving in to age, she had another, less clearly in mind, to do with using her outward appearance to hide her inward condition. For this purpose, she must be careful to underplay her part, to avoid excessive bright-ness of manner.

Shorty knocked, let the doctor in and cleared off as quickly as he could. He and Marigold had said the minimum to each other since the drink-spilling incident, which had come, so to speak, on top of her version of the Pusscat-drenching incident. But he would prepare and take in the coffee and biscuits, because Adela would be told if he failed to and because it was one of the things he did.

Marigold and the doctor asked and answered a couple of ques-tions about how each had spent Christmas. Her answers laid stress on the visit of her grandchildren and great-grandchildren. Then he said,

'Miss Bastable told me something about a fainting attack. How long were you unconscious?'

'Well, to be perfectly honest with you, I'm not absolutely sure I was ever what you'd call *unconscious* for a single moment. I'd had much more to eat and drink than an old lady like myself should have done, and I just had a sort of fit of dizziness.'

'I see. Have you experienced such attacks before?'

'Oh really, I think *attacks* is rather overstating the case. Miss Bastable was making a mountle-pountle out of a molehill; she fusses over me like an old hen.'

The doctor again said that he saw, established that his patient had felt perfectly well in the meantime, and warned her against any kind of undue—

'Yes, yes, yes, I understand that.'

Dr Mainwaring smoothed his moustache and asked about lapses of memory.

After five seconds, Marigold said slowly, 'I don't *think* they've got any worse. Oh, now and then I forget this or that, of course, but not often enough to bother me frightfully.'

Even if not already alerted by the excessive brightness of his patient's manner, the doctor would have concluded without much trouble, after that overdone pause, that something was being kept from him. But, short of scopolamine, hypnosis or wild horses, he knew he would never hear from her what it was; not that that was an important deprivation.

He thought of these and related matters while he asked about the tranquillizing pills, was told they were a great help, and wrote out a prescription for more. At this stage Shorty brought in the refreshments and again took himself off at top speed, hardly waiting to be tunkalunked. The doctor refused biscuits, having recognized at least one of those on the plate from his previous visit. After a sip of coffee, which tasted all right but smelt strange, he said,

'How's Miss Bastable keeping? I'm afraid I shan't be—'

'Oh, she's fine, she never complains. Adela's as strong as an ox.'

'She certainly has a remarkable—'

'She's such a worker. She did the whole of our Christmas practically on her own, and we were . . . yes, we were eleven at table, including the two tots. My grandchildren were here for the day with their respective spouses, do you see, and there were the two great-grandchildren as well.'

'Yes, I see.'

Thirty-Six

In George's bedroom – it was not one of his downstairs days – the doctor said,

'I'm delighted to hear it, Professor Zeyer. When you say total . . .'

'Let's put it that when running through any given category in my thoughts I've yet to come across an object I can't name, and I've been through plenty of categories. Door, knob, hinge, lintel, jamb, panel, window, frame, catch, pane, sash, cord, glass, dressing-table—'

'Yes, I see what you—'

'—drawer, handle, mirror, clothes-brush, hair-brush, comb, dressing-gown, cord, pocket, table, lamp, bulb, switch, flex, plug, socket . . .'

By saying slowly and continuously and more and more loudly that it was very interesting and quite remarkable and most extraordinary and much to be welcomed, Dr Mainwaring brought about silence at last. He delivered a warning against overexertion, trying to sound serious and yet not sepulchral, trying conscientiously too to make it appear that he had never uttered any such warning in his life before, then took his leave and went down to the kitchen.

Shorty was not to be seen at first, only the evidence of his labours: a large pan of some vegetable soup simmering gently, a smaller pan of potatoes, an opened tin of corned beef, two peeled Spanish onions on a board. The doctor tried to imagine what it must be like to live in this house, but did not have to do so for long, because after the sound of a w.c. being flushed and an outside door being slammed shut, Shorty entered the room buttoning his flies.

'Do I take it that thou cravest audience with thy unworthy servant, O mighty bearer of the staff of Hippocrates?'

'Just a very brief word, Mr Shortell, while I'm here. How are you?'

'Fine, how's yourself? No, I'm all right, doc, thank you kindly. Bowels well and truly open, as you may not unnaturally have surmised, no doubt in response to generous lashings of vino. Troubled by dandruff and fallen arches, but no bits broken off recently.'

'No change of any sort?'

'No,' said Shorty without hesitation, having already decided that the pants-pissing incident was too minor to be worth a mention, and wanting to end the talk so that he could take a drink in peace. But inquisitiveness made him ask, 'How's her nibs, then?'

'I'm sorry?'

'Mrs Mairygeld Pake.'

'Quite well on the whole, but she does seem a little strained. She needs, let's say bearing with.'

Strained arse through a lifetime of sitting on it, thought Shorty, and what she needs is a red-hot pokie-wokie up same. He said, 'Right. If you want the brigadier he'll be in the sitting-room.'

Thirty-Seven

The brigadier's location was as notified. Although at the windows and looking out, he took in little of what he saw. That day he had been restless, unable to settle down even to doing nothing. The doctor came in and Bernard turned to face him.

'Good morning, Mr Bastable . . . Any change?'

'Nothing dramatic. I seem to be passing rather more blood.'

'The haemorrhoids?'

'A great nuisance.'

'What about the pain?'

'I can stand it at the moment.'

'You're sure you don't want surgery? I could—'

'Brownjohn put my chances at less than five per cent. That's good enough for me.'

'You wouldn't like a second opinion?'

'According to you, Brownjohn's one of the very best in London, and having seen him I accept that view. So no. Thank you.'

'Mr Bastable, when . . . when this phase seems like coming to an end, I'd be grateful if you'd warn me in good time. I may not be able to find you a bed immediately.'

'A week?'

'Yes, that would be about right.'

'Very well. Goodbye, Dr Mainwaring.'

He held out his hand and the doctor, rather surprised, shook it.

'Goodbye, Mr Bastable.' Then, because it was every cinematic doctor's exit line, the doctor added, 'I'll see myself out.'

Left alone, Bernard arranged a cushion on one of Adela's tapestry chairs, sat down carefully, and lit a cigarette. When told that he had about three months left to him he had thought he could be brave, that he would be borne up by his own fortitude in not revealing his state and in never complaining, and that a show of steady affection to the others would not be too difficult, if only in that it might cause them to admire him in retrospect. So matters had seemed all the way back from Harley Street – he had taken the taxi that night in order to have more time to consider. But he had not been able to keep it up; perhaps he could have if he had been able to drink again, though he doubted it. Anyway, his only relief, and that a mild, transient one, had turned out to lie in malicious schemes, acts and remarks.

He had sat long enough; he got up stiffly and returned to the window. Outside, the sun was shining on various items of vegetation. Another mistaken forecast of his had been that, knowing what he knew, he would come to prize the things outside himself, like the scene before him; yet another, that he would have been able to look back on his life and – not find a meaning in it, which he had never hoped for, but see it as a whole. That might have been some compensation for having had to be Bernard Bastable, for having had to live.

There was the sound of Adela's car returning. He limped quickly off towards the kitchen in confident hope of an opportunity to ridicule and distress her.

Thirty-Eight

Nothing much was ever made of New Year's Eve at Tuppenny-hapenny Cottage, and the one that fell soon after Dr Mainwaring's visit turned out to be rather less convivial than was customary. Shortly went off to bed at his usual time, a few minutes before eleven, not because he wanted to avoid company but out of drunken prudence: he knew that to go on boozing for an extra hour and a half or more would appreciably worsen his hangover and also further afflict his guts, which since Christmas had been as irritable as he could remember. (Not to have gone on boozing and to have boozed less hard earlier were alike out of the question.) Bernard followed at an interval sufficient to guarantee Shorty's being in bed and asleep. He pleaded a headache; in fact, he was not quite sure how he would behave when that midnight struck.

So it was only Adela and Marigold who joined George in his bedroom at ten to twelve; it had been another of his upstairs days.

'1973,' he said reflectively. 'I find the years are sounding more and more odd. 1973 sounds like a thing out of those comics, with death-rays and robots and monsters from outer space. Whereas the year I was born sounds like stage-coaches and highwaymen and crinolines and fans and duelling-pistols and warming-pans and snuff-boxes and ruffles and shoe-buckles and—'

'I know what you mean,' said Marigold.

'Oh, you feel like that too, do you? How very—'

'No, but I know what you mean.'

'It seems a long time ago.' Adela did not phrase or pitch it as a question, but it was one.

'Doesn't it just?' said George. 'But the way to look at it, we ought to think of it as a victory. Another year without the Reds coming over with their tanks and armoured cars and tommy-guns and barbed wire and guard-dogs and watch-towers and—'

'Shall we put the wireless on?' asked Marigold. 'We want to make sure we're tuned in to the right station.'

With a practised movement, George stretched out his left hand and turned a switch. They heard sounds as of an immense assemblage that might have been a football crowd, an undisciplined but good-natured political congress, a drinks party or some other thing, with a band playing in the background and small groups of people talking loudly in the foreground. These constantly changed, in every case before any of the three listeners had had time to pick up the drift of what was being said, or even who was saying it. But quite soon there were calls for silence at whatever distant place it was, and Big Ben chimed twelve, and *Auld Lang Syne* began.

George switched off after a few bars. 'Well, that seems to be it. Happy New Year, and blessings on you both, and thank you for all you've done for me over the past twelve months and before.'

'Happy New Year,' said Marigold and Adela together.

The trio clinked glasses in turn, glasses holding some of the last of the rather good Chianti that Keith or Trevor had brought at Christmas. There was no further demonstration: Adela knew that no one liked being kissed by her, and George could not reach up to kiss either of the women, and Marigold realized that to kiss George and not kiss Adela would hurt Adela. But each was, if not exactly happy, at any rate content. Marigold was done with decisions for good. George was pretty sure by now that no editor or publisher was interested in any article or book he might produce; nevertheless he would continue to write. Adela looked forward to a year that, in her eyes, held no threat of change.

Thirty-Nine

'I must be off,' said Adela on the Friday morning of that week. 'They said the sooner I take the car into the garage the sooner they'll be finished with it.'

'It sounds logical,' said Bernard. 'When will you be back? In case anyone comes or anything.'

'As soon as they've finished with the car I'll start for home.'

'When will you be back?'

'They've got to change all the oil, do you see, and make sure the tyres are all right, and clean things in the engine and so on.'

'Yes, and so forth into the bargain I shouldn't wonder. For the love of God, when will you be back?'

'Oh, honestly . . . About six, I should think.'

'Six-thirtyish. Don't forget the *Telegraph*.'

'I won't.'

They nodded at each other and Adela left. She was looking forward to her day in Newmarket: necessary shopping soon done, then a look round the sales, lunch in a café, perhaps a cinema if she could find a film not certain to be wholly incomprehensible to her. It would have been ten times as much fun if Marigold were coming too, but she had decided against it at the last minute, saying she felt she needed rest.

Bernard poured himself a third cup of coffee and lit a cigarette, though he felt no need of either except as providing activity of a sort. The w.c. sounded nearby and Shorty came in, wriggling slightly and frowning.

'Toimes ya could bar a door wid ut,' he said, 'and toimes ya could sop ut wid a spewn. It's a sopping day today all right. That was my third. Oof! Bernard, didn't you use to have some kind of liquid cement stuff that gummed your guts up? I don't hold with messing about with your insides as a rule, but I'm getting a bit—'

'In my top left-hand drawer, green leather case with two bottles. You want the one with the white liquid in it. Don't touch the other, the clear liquid: it's a very powerful aperient. Remember – the white liquid.'

'What sort of dose?'

'Well, I should say about a tablespoonful as a start, then see how it is in three to four hours.'

'Heartfelt thanks.'

Shorty left the kitchen and made towards the stairs, then reconsidered. He was nearly sure that there remained some of the Scotch brought by Trevor or Keith – a natural ring-tightener, Scotch, better than any medicine, and drunk-making too. The sitting-room was empty. What he sought stood on the tile-topped table, a couple of inches of it or more. He considered again, but not for long, and emptied the bottle in a series of sips, coughing happily.

In the meantime, Bernard had gone to the dresser, brought out two small bags of transparent plastic and stuffed them in his pocket. He slipped quietly into the garden; it was a mild morning for the time of year and he did not expect to have to stay long out of doors. So it proved: quite soon, near the box hedge, he found a respectable pile of Mr Pastry's turds. With his back towards the house, he lowered himself by painful stages until he was squatting on his heels, produced the plastic bags, put his right hand into one and held the other open. His plan was to dump the excrement in some sensitive area of the cottage, such as Marigold's bed, and so escalate his campaign for the removal of the dog and the distressing of George. But (Bernard asked himself now) what would be the point? He saw that George's state of mind, his happiness or unhappiness, had become, as if at that moment, perfectly indifferent to him. The next moment, it dawned on him that, after that first hit with the water-pistol and two or three partial successes later, he had let Pusscat go unscathed. He stood up, again by degrees, dropped the bags on the wet grass and went back indoors.

Marigold was in the sitting-room, engaged on a petit-point cushion-cover for Rachel's birthday. Since Christmas, reversing an earlier policy, she had started to spend some hours of every day here. Her own company held less appeal than it once had; she wrote fewer letters, because she was afraid of sending the same person the same news twice over or more, and it was tiresome to make and keep copies; she felt she had better try to be sociable with Bernard and Shorty, on whose good will she must depend increasingly, while at the same time not conceding that either possessed any good will.

The door thudded open and Bernard came in. He sat down slowly on his rocking-chair, lit a cigarette and picked up the *Radio Times*.

'You look pale, Bernard,' said Marigold truthfully. 'I think you smoke too much. It can't do you any good at your age.'

'Nor any harm either. I'm all right.'

'I wish Trevor would ring up.'

'Is there any particular reason why he should?'

'I mean Keith. They're having that meeting today, the one to decide, you know, about the pet-food advertisement. He promised he'd telephone the *moment* he heard the result.'

'I'm sure he will.' Bernard's mind was picking up speed. He saw what he would have to do, regardless of whether he wanted to do it or what would follow; not to do it would amount to total surrender.

After a thoughtful puff or two, he said, 'I must admit I rather hope those vandals don't take it into their heads to pay us a visit.'

'Vandals?'

'The ones who've been smashing up places in the village.' Trying to feel pride and triumph in his conduct of the manoeuvre, he went on, 'You were telling me about it – when was it? – yesterday.'

'Was I? Oh, those people, yes. Little swine. Still, we're a long way out.'

'That could cut both ways. No neighbours.'

'If we stand up to them they'll just cut and run. Bullies are always cowards; everyone knows that.'

Bernard was on the point of voicing his sincere doubt of this proposition when Shorty came in, as was customary, with coffee and biscuits – cheaper and nastier, if fresher, biscuits than the ones offered Dr Mainwaring. When he had served the other two, Shorty sat down and served himself. After more than three years, Marigold still found this unsettling. It was as if one of those foreign waiters at the Café Royal should have pulled up a chair next to her and started on the grouse and burgundy. But she was not to be unsettled for long: after a sip of coffee, Shorty excused himself and hurried from the room.

'Right,' he said, once more emerging from the outside lavatory – 'cement, here I come.'

Up in Bernard's half of the bedroom, a spot he visited not once a year, he looked to see if there had been any changes or additions. No: water-carafe and tumbler, clean silver ashtray on small wine-table by bedside, silver pen-and-ink set on chest of drawers, and that was the lot. He, Bernard, had thrown everything away; Shorty himself had never kept anything.

The green leather case came to hand readily enough and the two bottles were there, each of them surrounded with a label worn and faded into illegibility. As if in response, his guts, seldom altogether silent, intensified their stirrings. The effect was of an acoustic recording of a thunderstorm played on an acoustic gramophone.

'You look out, you lot,' he said: 'heap big chief him coming to put paid to palaver.' He picked up the glass and poured into it a little of the contents of one of the bottles: a transparent fluid. In Shorty's world, transparent fluids were called white, notably white (as opposed to yellow) gin, white (as opposed to caramel-coloured) whisky. He was not very sober, and he had forgotten Bernard's caution about the clear liquid. So he poured again, making up a dose of about two tablespoonfuls, and drank it down.

'Ugh,' he said. 'Well, we all know it won't do you any good if it's not bloody horrible. That's life. By the great bull of Bashan, that is life for you. I reckon God was pissed when he made the world and he's had a screaming hangover ever since. Wow.'

Bernard too had left the sitting-room and was now in the coal-house looking through the detached drawer in which Shorty kept a stock of largely corroded tools. He searched through them with mounting fervour until he found an implement of the type he needed. Time was not on his side; he wanted very much to act now, but knew he must wait until the afternoon, when the other two would have retired.

On her way upstairs to wash her hands before luncheon, Marigold noticed Mr Pastry's tennis-ball lying in shadow on the second tread from the top. She left it where it was, saying to herself idly that it would do one or the other of those two no harm to tread on it and take a bit of a toss.

They ate a cold meal in the kitchen, George a portion of the same in his bedroom. Bernard returned to the sitting-room and chain-smoked until all was quiet, really impatient, the vestiges of his imagination caught by the task-force, behind-the-lines aspect of what he was about to do. Finally he crept into the garden, trampled some flower-beds and pulled up a number of plants – this to lend colour to the vandalism theory he would later advance. When he came out of the coal-house carrying the ladder, he did not hear a fairly loud groan and a spluttering sound from near by. The daylight had just begun to fade. Bernard, wincing with pain and effort, propped the ladder against the far side of the house and laboriously mounted it. At the top, he reached up and cut the telephone wire with the pair of pliers he had found, laughed with great abandonment, lost his balance and fell.

He had broken something, something large. There was also a lot of what must be blood. Crying out with pain now, he crawled a little way, just far enough to be out of sight of anyone approaching the front door of the cottage, and found he could crawl no further.

A little later, Marigold went upstairs to the lavatory. This time, in the thicker shadows, she did not notice the tennis-ball, and did not remember having done so before when she began her descent. Her foot came down squarely on it and both her legs seemed snatched into the air. She went full tilt, not stopping until her forehead came into contact with the heavy brass rim of the log-basket in the hall.

George was asleep, heavily because he had been awake, as usual, since about six o'clock that morning, but the sound from downstairs reached him. He pulled himself upright and shouted at the top of his voice for several minutes; there was no response. With great exertion, he worked his way out of bed and on to the floor. Then nothing happened for a time.

When he recovered consciousness, he was stretched on the landing in almost complete darkness with Mr Pastry at his side. He tried to shout again, but could not, tried to move, but could not. All he could do was turn his eyes this way and that. He felt no fear: whether or nor the other three returned soon from wherever they had gone, Adela was bound to arrive eventually in her car. Yes, her car, with its wheels, tyres, axles, windows, gear-lever, dashboard . . . So he still had that.

Adela drove along the side of the house, her headlights just missing Bernard's corpse by the wall. As she approached the back door, she heard a strange noise a few feet away, hesitated, found the door of the lavatory unbolted and was aware of a smell that was worse than strange. She groped for the light-switch. Shorty had fallen off the w.c. seat and was lying in a considerable pool of brownish water with long streaks of dark blood in it. Adela walked a few unsteady paces, felt her way into the kitchen, then the hall, turned on the light there and saw Marigold.

'Oh, my dearest, whatever have you done to yourself?' she said in a thicker voice than usual. She was aware of something like a huge weight against her chest, and then of nothing at all.

Forty

Nobody except the postman, who noticed nothing out of the ordinary, came to Tuppenny-hapenny Cottage for several days, because nobody else had reason to: no milkman arrived to find bottles not taken in, no shopkeeper missed Adela's custom, and Keith, having conscientiously tried to telephone his wife's grandmother with news of his success and failed to get through, had assumed that Adela had once more neglected to pay the bill and been cut off. So he wrote a letter instead.

At the end of those days, a large red car bearing the name of a hire firm came laboriously up the drive. It stopped at the front door and its hooter sounded for a minute or so. Then a man in his thirties, wearing a suit of some shiny material rarely seen thereabouts, opened the driver's door.

'I'll take a look around in back,' he said in a North American accent.

'Okay, Stanley,' said his companion, a woman of about his age. 'But hurry it up, will you? I'm not exactly cooking to death.'

The man nodded and walked slowly along to the angle of the house. Here he saw a ladder leaning against the wall, a metal tool near its foot and a fallen telephone wire. Frowning, he moved to his right and walked on more slowly still; then his eye fell on what might have been a heap of sacking three-quarters covered with windblown leaves, except that it had a trousered human leg and a shoed foot sticking out of it. The new arrival drew in his breath, stooped quickly and brushed away the leaves until he had uncovered a face. Because it was a face he knew only from photographs and the dimmest of infantile memory, he did not at once recognize it.

OTHER NEW YORK REVIEW CLASSICS

For a complete list of titles, visit www.nyrb.com or write to:
Catalog Requests, NYRB, 435 Hudson Street, New York, NY 10014

* *Also available as an electronic book.*